To Carter

MUST LOVE PETS

Dog's Best Friend

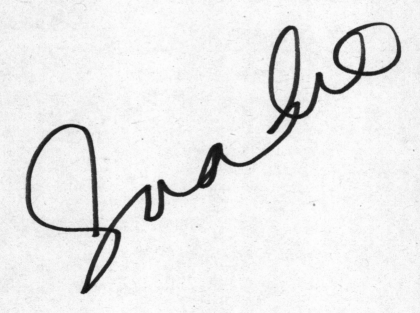

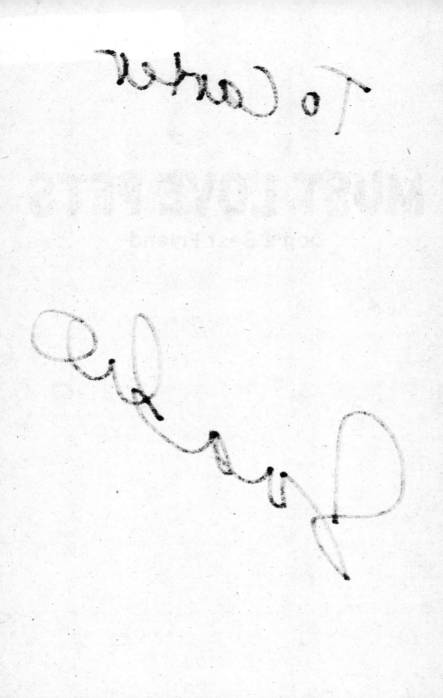

MUST LOVE PETS

Dog's Best Friend

Saadia Faruqi

SCHOLASTIC INC.

ISBN 978-1-338-78351-3

10 9 8 7 6 5 4 3 2 1   23 24 25 26 27

Printed in the U.S.A. 40

First printing 2023

Book design by Omou Barry

In memory of Zubair Mamoo

1951–1991

CHAPTER 1

My best friend London Harrison is ah-mazing. She's supersmart and always calm and collected. That's why when she rushes into my house one afternoon like her hair's on fire, I get worried.

"Guess what, Imaan!" she says, panting.

I'm sitting on my bed, surrounded by books I'm supposed to be reading. Our fifth-grade English teacher, Mrs. Levite, said it's especially important to read during summer break. Something about our brains turning to mush if we let the entire summer go by without books.

Only it's hard to find something that's not totally

boring. Maybe I'll ask Dada Jee to take me to the library soon.

London flops down on my bed right on top of the books. "C'mon, guess!" she moans, like she just can't hold in her news.

"You won the lottery?"

She gives me a wry look. "Um, no. Try again."

I poke her with my foot. "My brain is turning to mush. I can't think."

She sits up quickly. "Okay, remember my uncle Tommy?"

I nod, even though London has a hundred relatives. I've only a vague idea who this Uncle Tommy is. Someone youngish who wears glasses, I think. "Did *he* win the lottery?" I ask.

"What? No! He's got a new dog!" She pauses. "Maybe that's kind of like winning the lottery, but that's not the story here."

"Okay . . . ?" I'm not sure why London is telling me this unless it's to rub in the fact that I, Imaan Bashir, extreme dog lover, still don't have one of my own. It's my lifelong dream to be a dog owner, but Mama refuses to discuss it. She's so against it that she's given me forty-three nos already.

London is looking at me with a wide grin but also a little eye roll like she thinks I'm clueless. "He's also got a new job . . ."

I smack her on the arm. "Brain turning to mush, remember? Hurry up with the story before I fall asleep."

She smacks my arm back. "His new job is sending him to Las Vegas for training, and he's asked me to take care of Candy."

"Candy?" I repeat.

"The dog. She's named Candy."

I think about this. Uncle Tommy has a new dog. And a new job. And he's asked London to take care of the dog while he takes care of the job. "But you've got Boots," I finally say. "Your evil cat."

I'm not even kidding. Boots is an old, cranky tabby that scratches anyone who gets close. And she absolutely hates dogs. Like, hissing, glaring, and even spitting at any dog that comes near her.

"That's why I think Candy should be our client instead," London says, grinning some more.

My heart starts pounding. It's been a few weeks since we last took in a client for our pet-sitting business Must Love Pets. We've taken care of dogs, goats, kittens, rabbits, and even a talking parakeet. It was the best kind of fun and chaos. But after our last client, things slowed down for a bit, and I was thankful. We all needed the rest. Searching for escaped animals and cleaning up destroyed property makes for a highly stressful business.

Plus, Mama was about to have a panic attack due to

all the animals running around the Bashir house like they owned the place.

"Tell me more about this . . . Candy," I say. She sounds like the perfect way to get back to pet sitting. Also, the whole point of Must Love Pets is to prove to Mama how responsible I can be. How ready I am to have a dog of my own.

"Let's call a team meeting," London replies. "If we're taking on a new client, all of us should be here."

She means our other best friend, Olivia, who recently moved to California. We met on her first day in the neighborhood and instantly became friends. She knows a lot about animals already, and she's a big help with figuring things out when it all starts going nuts at Must Love Pets. "Good idea," I say. "I'll call her."

Then I stop because I'm not sure how to do that. None of us have our own phones, so we have to rely on landlines like it's the 1900s. Only I have no idea what Olivia's home number is. "Drat."

London scrambles up from the bed. "Let's go," she says. "We can chat at her place."

We head downstairs quickly. I'm hoping we can sneak out the door without alerting anyone, but it's no use. Mama is in the living room, hurling Legos into their box like she's mad at them or something.

"Wow, that's a lot of Legos," London mutters to me.

It's true. They're scattered all over the floor, and a few piles are on the couch too. It looks like a Lego monster vomited all over our living room. Mama's literally scowling . . . so basically her usual expression. I wonder if she looks like that when she's sleeping too.

"What was that?" Mama asks, looking up at me.

Oops. Did I say that out loud?

"What's going on, Mrs. Bashir?" London asks hurriedly.

Mama sighs and waves her arms around. "What do you think? There's a mess that needs to be cleaned up."

London joins her on the floor and starts helping. I look around for the culprit. Sure enough, my six-year-old brother, Amir, is sitting on the couch, his arms folded on his chest. He's scowling too, but he looks adorable. "I want to play with them," he insists, sniffing a little.

I gulp. Every time Amir sniffs or sneezes, I worry that his allergies are back. He first got them when our neighbor's dog, Sir Teddy, came to stay with us. He also sneezed a lot when we took him to the farmers' market and met the cutest goat, Marmalade. But we've had other clients that never made Amir sneeze. It's a mystery London is determined to solve.

"You've played enough," Mama says grimly. "They've been lying around since last night, and I keep stepping on them."

"But . . ."

"Come on, buddy!" I grab Amir's hand and pull him up. "Let's help clean this up quickly."

He kicks a Lego. "No!"

"It'll be fun!" I cajole. "If you hurry, I'll take you to the park."

He stops scowling. "Can I go on the swings?"

"Sure!"

"You don't have to do that," Mama says quickly. "Your dada will be home from the grocery store in a little while."

Dada Jee is Baba's dad, and it's his main job to look after Amir while Mama works. But he's old and grumpy, so sometimes Amir gets to be too much for him. "That's okay," I say cheerfully. "We'll have fun in the park."

London's mouth falls open. "Really?"

I get it. I'm always complaining about Amir tagging along and ruining our girl time. But I don't like Mama's stressed-looking face at all. Hanging out with Amir is a good trade for relaxing her a little bit. After all, we have to convince her to let us keep Candy. Even though Must Love Pets is ours, Mama has final say on clients staying here.

"Yeah, really," I reply. "Let's have our team meeting at the park instead."

Mama looks up. "Another client?" she asks, eyebrows raised.

Oops. Pet-sitting clients are another thing that stresses her out. I offer her a little smile. "Maybe?"

London nods her head. "Definitely."

"Another animal?" Amir breathes. "Which one? I want kittens again; they were the best!"

"Clean up first, then you can get the details," I say sternly. He kneels on the carpet and quickly gets to work. His hands are a blur as he grabs Lego pieces and throws them into the box.

Mama takes a deep breath and stands up. "Okay, thanks, girls. Make sure this room is clean before you head out."

"Sure, Mrs. Bashir," says London.

Amir throws the last Lego into the box, then stands up straight and salutes. "Aye, aye, Captain!"

London and I roll our eyes at each other, but we're smiling too. Even Mama can't help but smile. "Be good and don't bother your sister or her friends," she tells him.

He's already running to the hallway to put on his shoes. "I'm always good!" he shouts back. "I'm the goodest."

Yeah, right.

CHAPTER 2

A few minutes later, we walk to the neighborhood park. London stops to knock on Olivia's door nearby.

Amir is too impatient. "Come on, there's always a long line for the swings!" He drags me straight toward the park entrance. It's a little gate that's supposed to stay locked but currently stands wide open.

"Kids!" I grumble under my breath, then realize I sound just like Dada Jee.

The park is full of people. I'm not exaggerating. There are kids everywhere, running around on the grass and jumping in the playground. A few parents hang out too, taking care of little ones, but it's mostly the older neighborhood kids.

"It's like they let all the kids out of prison . . . ahem, school."

I turn around at the sound of Olivia's voice. "Summer break equals freedom," I agree.

We give one another hugs. I even hug London, who I just saw a few minutes ago. We giggle a little at how silly we're being, but that's the best part about our friendship. We can be silly and weird, but we're still besties.

"The swings, Imaan!" Amir whines and pulls my hand.

I let him lead me to the swings behind the playground. They're a long set of four in a row, and as expected, they're all taken. Amir pouts. "I wanna . . ."

"Don't worry," I say quickly. "We'll just stand here until someone leaves."

He opens his mouth to protest, then a miracle

happens. He nods and says, "Okay," like it's no big deal. I wait for a tantrum, but it never happens.

London, Olivia, and I exchange looks. "Wow," London whispers.

Olivia ruffles Amir's hair. "Proud of you, buddy," she says. "Why don't you look for acorns or something? They're all over the place."

"Acorns are for babies," he tells her, sinking down to the grass. "How about slugs?"

"Ew, but okay," she replies.

I forget about Amir and his grossness and turn to London. "So?"

She raises her eyebrows. "So what?"

"Very funny," I say. "Candy."

Olivia frowns. "We're eating candy? Pretty sure your mom wouldn't like Amir to have any."

"Candy's a dog," I tell her. "And apparently our next client."

"Ooh, tell me!" Olivia squeals. "I've been waiting for another dog."

This is true. Olivia loves dogs as much as I do. London launches into the story of her uncle Tommy. Then she describes Candy. She's a Yorkshire terrier, which means small, cute, and very high energy.

I sigh. "Sounds perfect."

Olivia is more practical. "How long will she stay with us?"

That's how all Must Love Pets team meetings are. I get excited about the animals, and London and Olivia pull me back to reality with boring details. But I don't mind. It's why our business works so well. We all have skills that complement one another.

That's just a fancy way of saying we each have an important role to play in the business.

"A few days," London replies to Olivia.

Olivia frowns. "You don't know how many

exactly? That's the first thing we ask clients."

"Well, Uncle Tommy didn't actually contact Must Love Pets," London admits. "He wanted me to take care of her myself, but you know Boots."

Actually, Olivia's never met Boots. "What do you mean?" she asks.

London just shakes her head. "You'll see," she mutters darkly.

Olivia looks at me questioningly.

"Devil cat," I tell her.

Olivia laughs. "Come on, she can't be that bad."

"Uh, yeah, she can," London says. "One time she shredded all the curtains in our living room because we disturbed her nap."

I giggle. "I remember. We were in third grade. We were watching movies in that room all Saturday. Really loud too!"

"Boots hates noise," London explains.

"And people. And animals. And too much light . . ."
I take a huge breath because I have a whole list of things
Boots dislikes enough to hiss and scratch at.

Olivia holds up her hand. "Okay, I get it. Candy
can't stay there."

"Exactly."

Just then, Amir scrambles up and starts to run
toward the swings. A kid is just getting off, which
means it's Amir's turn. "Imaan, help me!" he yells as
he runs.

I sigh and follow him slowly. This kid and his
dramatics. He's perfectly capable of getting on and off
swings by himself. I help him on, then give a big push.

"Higher!" he demands.

"You know how to push yourself," I say sternly.

He probably pouts or something, but I'm standing
behind him, so I don't see. "Have fun!" I call out. Then
I turn and stride back to my friends.

Must Love Pets needs to get ready for a new animal.

It's almost time to head back home. London, Olivia, and I are sitting at our favorite picnic table at the back of the park. Typically, we'd lie down side by side on top of the table, with our legs dangling down to the ground. But today we have Amir, who's playing with a few other kids in the sandbox nearby. I need to keep an eye on him because he can get into trouble in the blink of an eye.

Literally.

"Isn't that your dad, Olivia?" London points to a spot near the fence. Sure enough, Mr. Gordon and two other burly men are digging up the soil with shovels. "What are they doing?"

Olivia nods. "He's the new president of the neighborhood beautification committee."

My eyes widen. "What is that?" I ask.

She shrugs. "They make sure nothing gets dirty or broken around the neighborhood. Keep the streets clean. Make everything look pretty."

I squint. "What are they doing here?"

"Planting trees, I think. My dad said this whole section near the fence has been empty for a long time. It needs some change."

I swallow. It's true. There's been nothing in this part of the park for many years.

London frowns. "Has it always been like that? Really?"

Olivia shrugs again because obviously she has no idea. She just moved here. But I know. "There used to be a bench here," I whisper.

London turns to me. "Hmm, are you sure?"

Of course I'm sure. "I used to sit there with Baba all the time," I say quietly. "After playing, when I'd get tired, he'd bring me to that bench and feed me carrots and water. Sometimes orange juice."

London snaps her fingers. "Oh, that's right. I do remember a bench!" But her voice lowers, like she's nervous.

I give her a quick smile. I'm used to people getting nervous when I talk about my baba. He died of brain cancer when I was six years old. I should be used to him being gone, but I'm really not. I miss him so much. But that's not even the worst part. The worst part is that nobody wants to talk about him. Not my friends, not even my family.

It would be awful if I forgot about Baba just because nobody remembered him anymore. So no matter how weird people feel, I talk about him every chance I get.

I keep staring at Mr. Gordon and his friends. They're digging so hard that tiny clumps of mud fly everywhere. If I focus, I can almost see the exact place the bench used to be. Right in front of a big knot on the fence. Sometimes I'd turn around and trace the knot with my fingers. Baba would always pull my hand away, saying, *You'll get splinters if you're not careful*, jaan.

Only I was six years old, and I had no clue what splinters were.

Then one day I got a splinter in my finger from that knot in the fence. I bawled just like Amir does now. Ha! But Baba never said *I told you so.* He just hugged me.

I feel arms go around me in a hug. But it's not Baba this time. It's London. "You okay?" she whispers.

I nod because yes, I am. These are good memories. They keep Baba alive in my heart.

London squeezes me again, then lets me go. Olivia pats me on the shoulder and says in a bubbly voice. "So, when is Candy arriving?"

I guess emotional time is over. That's okay. I'm ready for some animal time instead.

CHAPTER 3

Early the next morning, I head to London's house. She's my next-door neighbor, even though the entrance to the park lies between our two houses.

London's mom opens the door. She's dressed in a yellow pantsuit, so I guess she's leaving for work soon. It's only eight o'clock and I haven't even had breakfast yet, but I flash my best smile. "Hello, Mrs. Harrison."

She smiles back as I walk inside. "Hello, Imaan. How's your mama? I haven't seen her in forever."

I highly doubt it. Mama and Mrs. Harrison are besties just like London and me. Even if they don't meet in person, they're always texting and chatting on the phone. "She's fine," I reply. "Busy with work as usual."

"She works too hard."

"Tell me about it." I stop in the hallway because I suddenly have a brilliant idea. "Why don't you two go somewhere? Just to relax and have fun?"

Mrs. Harrison stops too. "What, like a vacation? Young lady, you know neither of us has time for that nonsense."

Just then, London and Olivia appear at the top of the stairs. "Hey, Imaan!" London calls out. She's dressed in her favorite clothes: white jeans with a white T-shirt, plus a navy-blue suit jacket that makes her look like a businesswoman.

I, on the other hand, am wearing black sweatpants and a crumpled green T-shirt from yesterday. What can I say? I'm not an early-morning person, especially not on summer break.

"You're late," London says. "Uncle Tommy's gonna be here soon."

I raise a finger. "Wait a minute." Then I turn back to Mrs. Harrison because this is absolutely an important conversation we're having. "Not a vacation," I tell her. "Like a weekend getaway or something. We're old enough to take care of ourselves, right, London?"

"What are you talking about?" she asks.

"I think our moms need a weekend getaway."

Olivia claps her hands. "Ooh, my mom too. She never takes a break."

I give Mrs. Harrison a pleading look. "What do you think? Mama will only go for it if you insist."

She laughs a little. "Maybe. We'll see."

When a grown-up says *we'll see*, it usually means *probably not* instead. I narrow my eyes at her, wondering how I can change her mind. "Sure," I finally say. "We'll talk more about this later."

Mrs. Harrison picks up her purse and turns away. "I'm leaving for work, girls. Make sure you go back to Imaan's soon."

We all nod. We're not supposed to stay alone, so London usually hangs out at my place when her parents are at work. "Don't worry, Mom," London tells her. "We'll leave as soon as Uncle Tommy brings Candy."

We don't have long to wait. Uncle Tommy arrives just a few minutes after London's mom leaves. He's as nice as I remember, smiling as he lugs a pet carrier inside. "Well, hello there," he rumbles. "Are all of you here to meet my little dog?"

I try gazing into the pet carrier. "Just how little are we talking?" I ask.

He lets out a laugh. "Candy's not tiny or anything if that's what you're worried about."

"We love tiny dogs," Olivia assures him.

"We love all dogs," I add. "Whatever their size."

London leads us all to the living room. It's cozy, with couches the color of warm gold, and a low wooden coffee table. "Uncle Tommy," she begins, clasping her hands together. "We have something to tell you."

Wait, what?

I realize in that instant that she hasn't exactly explained Must Love Pets to him yet. "Seriously, London?" I hiss. What if he doesn't want to deal with us? What if he wants his precious dog to stay in London's house?

Uncle Tommy sets down the carrier and collapses on a couch. "What's up, baby girl?"

"See, Candy can't stay here because of Boots," she begins. "So, we decided to keep her at Imaan's house instead."

He frowns a little. "Who's Boots?" he asks. "And who's this Imaan?"

I raise my hand. "That's me. Imaan, I mean. Not Boots."

London opens her mouth to explain, but there's a streak of gray and a yowl that raises the hair on the back of my neck. "That's Boots," she says, sighing.

We all look toward the noise. Boots has come out of hiding. She usually sleeps underneath a little chair near the living room window. I'm guessing she loves the sunlight or something. Right now, she's jumped up on the chair and is staring at us with evil green eyes. Her mouth is open in a growl.

"Yikes," Olivia says, staring.

I take a nervous step backward. I can't help it. Boots is just a cat, I know. I'm supposed to be an animal lover. Someone who adores all creatures. But London's cat is something else. She's always big, but right now, her hair is like a bush, straight in the air. Even her tail is arrowed up toward the ceiling. She's one big, angry furball ready to scratch your eyes out if you take a wrong step.

Yikes indeed.

"Boots, stop!" London says gently. She's the only one of us who's not scared. I can hear whimpering from the pet carrier, and my heart goes out to poor Candy.

"Can we get her out of here?" Olivia asks nervously.

"Sure, good idea." London looks around. "We need a blanket."

There are zero blankets in the living room. I could get one from London's room, but Candy's whimpering is getting louder. I point to Uncle Tommy's blazer. "How about that?"

Uncle Tommy jumps up from the couch and shrugs out of the blazer at top speed. "Here!" He practically throws it at London.

She catches it and then walks carefully over to Boots. "Easy, tiger," she murmurs.

We all watch. It's obvious she's done this before. I

don't even want to know how many other animals—
and humans—Boots has terrified.

London wraps the cat in the blazer and takes her
out of the room. The bundle struggles and yowls, but
London is strong.

"Stay there!" London places the blazer-covered cat
in the hallway outside and pulls the door shut behind
her. There's more yowling and spitting from outside,
and then a scratching on the door.

"Yikes," Olivia says again.

"She'll stop soon," London tells us. "I hope."

"I forgot all about your cat," Uncle Tommy mumbles.

"How can anyone forget about that nightmare?"
Olivia says, shivering.

London shrugs. "It's no big deal. We're used to it."

Uncle Tommy scratches his chin and thinks for a
second. "Candy can't stay here," he finally declares.
"She gets scared very easily."

I peer into the carrier again, but I can't really see anything. This dog seems like a handful. Little. Scares easily. We've never had a client that wasn't playful and energetic. Candy seems the complete opposite.

The whimpering has stopped, at least. I want to hug her so badly. Or maybe, after seeing Boots, I'm the one who needs a hug.

Uncle Tommy puts his head in his hands. "What am I going to do now?" he groans. "I have to leave for Las Vegas this afternoon."

London straightens the sleeves of her suit jacket. "Let me tell you about Must Love Pets."

CHAPTER 4

It's decided. Candy will come to my house as an official pet-sitting client.

Uncle Tommy agrees to the plan almost instantly, which surprises me. He asks zero questions, just says, "Send me the bill in a text message," then rushes out of London's house like Boots is after him.

Since it's Boots we're talking about, the possibility definitely exists. She's got a nasty habit of lying in wait for her enemies and sneaking up on them when they least expect it. Once, she jumped on my shoelaces and tore them to shreds.

I try not to wear sneakers to London's house anymore.

We lug Candy's carrier up the street to my house. Or at least, London and I lug it. Olivia follows behind, chattering all the way. "Isn't it weird how your uncle rushed away, London?" she asks.

"He had a plane to catch," she replies.

"Isn't it also weird that he didn't want to know anything about our company?" Olivia continues. "Most clients have tons of questions. How much it will cost. How we'll take care of the pet. How much experience we have."

"So many questions!" I agree.

"He trusts me," London says. "He was already planning to leave Candy with me."

"Still," Olivia says. "Isn't it weird he didn't leave us with a bag or anything for Candy? Like, where are her toys? Her dog bed? Her treats?"

Hmm, that *is* weird. Uncle Tommy had handed

over a plastic bag with two cans of dog food. Nothing else. I stop walking and give London a sideways glance. "Maybe he forgot," I suggest.

London doesn't seem concerned. She keeps walking, pulling me with her. "Boots probably scared his good sense away," she says.

"Should we call him?" I ask.

"No need," London replies in her usual airy tone. "We can figure it out."

"Yes, but isn't it weird . . ." Olivia starts again.

"Shush, girl!" London snaps.

"But I'm just saying . . ."

Thankfully, we reach my house before my two besties have a fight over a dog we haven't even seen yet. If you ask me, that's the weirdest part of this entire situation. We've never taken on a new pet without a single idea of what she looks like.

Well, okay. London's seen her, so that's something.

"What's Candy like?" I ask as I let go of my side of the carrier to open the back door.

"She's cute," London replies. "You'll see."

That is *so* not helpful. I should have asked for pictures or something yesterday when London first told me about Candy.

We enter the kitchen, and London sets the carrier down on the floor carefully. I look around. Mama and Dada Jee are sitting at the kitchen table, mugs of tea in their hands. But if you think they're relaxing or even happy, you're mistaken. They're having a literal stare-down, like in a cowboy movie, only their weapons are tea mugs and ugly scowls.

"Absolutely not!" Mama says to Dada Jee firmly.

Dada Jee only grunts. I'm not surprised. It's his go-to sound for almost every topic of conversation. *Want dinner, Dada Jee?* Grunt. *How about some ice cream, Dada Jee?* Grunt. *Where's Amir, Dada Jee?* Grunt grunt grunt.

The good thing is, I've become an expert in grumpy speech. And right now, Dada Jee is not happy. "What's going on?" I ask cheerfully.

Dada Jee scowls at me from underneath bushy eyebrows. "Your mother thinks she can stop my friends from visiting."

I gasp in an exaggerated way. "Mama! How dare you?

Olivia giggles. London smirks because she's used to how I operate. Sometimes making fun of Mama and Dada Jee is the only way to get rid of the tension they seem to live under 24/7.

Dada Jee grunts again. Really.

Mama relaxes a little. She even rolls her eyes. "I'm not stopping a little visit. But I don't want a full-fledged get-together of all the neighborhood grandfathers in the middle of the day."

"Why not?" Olivia asks.

Mama stares at her like she's never met her before. "Excuse me?"

Olivia swallows. "I'm just asking," she says nervously. "Why can't the grandpas get together in the middle of the day? Like, would you prefer evening? Or night?"

"Olivia asks lots of questions," London says teasingly. "You get used to it after a while."

Mama shakes her head and turns back to Dada Jee. "I'm fine with your visitors," she tells him. "But I need quiet in the mornings to work. You know I'm using the living room these days."

Mama is an accountant. She usually works from the little office in the back of our house. But that room gets really hot in the summer, so she's been working from the living room and even the patio some days. I can see how a grandpa party in the middle of the day would mess with her schedule.

And her deadlines. Tax deadlines are absolutely

brutal. You don't want to mess with them, unless you want the IRS to come looking for you.

"How about in the afternoon, around four o'clock?" I quickly ask.

Dada Jee and Mama both look at me, surprised. I guess they can't believe I shut down their staring contest in less than a minute.

"That will work," Mama agrees.

Grunt.

I'm helping Mama clean up the breakfast leftovers when Amir comes running into the kitchen. "Can we go to the park again?" he shouts, breathless.

"Calm down, silly," I tell him. "We have a guest."

Everyone stares at me, then to the pet carrier I'm pointing at. "A guest?" Amir drops down on his knees and peers inside. "Who is it?"

Mama frowns. "I didn't even notice that."

"It's Candy, my uncle's dog," London explains. "We're going to keep her here for a few days."

"Oh, because of Boots?" Mama gives a little nod like it's obvious why Candy can't stay with London. Then she adds, "Your mom called me last night."

See, I knew they talk all the time! They're besties, after all.

"She's awfully quiet for a dog," Dada Jee says as if someone is playing a trick on him. "Are you sure it's not a turtle or something?"

Just then, we hear a little yelp. It's very low, almost like a question being asked in dog language. "What's she saying?" Amir asks.

"I think she's asking if she can come out," London replies. She kneels next to him and opens the carrier from the top. We all lean forward. All I can see is a ball of brown-and-black fluff, quivering slightly.

"Aww," Amir, Olivia, and I say together.

London carefully reaches inside and takes the ball of fluff in her arms. Then she stands up. Amir follows, standing very close to her, but staying still.

My heart thumps. The ball of fluff is absolutely adorable. I can see pointed ears, plus a tiny face with bright eyes and a wet nose. I sigh because I think I'm in love.

"Meet Candy," London says.

My hands itch to hold the precious fluff ball, but before I can do anything, Amir steps forward.

"Can I pet her?" he asks, his little body bridling with excitement.

London nods, and Amir starts to stroke his entire hand on Candy's head. I open my mouth to caution him, but Candy's expression doesn't change. "I guess she's a really chill dog, huh?"

"I've never met a dog that didn't bark at strangers," Dada Jee says suspiciously.

"Or get excited to see kids," Mama adds.

They both nod at each other wisely. It's hilarious to see them agreeing on something. But they're right because I've been wondering the same thing about Candy. How come she's so calm and quiet?

London shrugs. "Uncle Tommy says she's very inactive. He got her from the shelter just a few months ago, so he's not sure what the problem is."

"Maybe she's sick," Amir suggests, still stroking Candy's head. "Maybe her tummy is hurting. When my tummy hurts, I feel like closing my eyes and lying down somewhere all alone."

"That's because you've eaten too much ice cream," I say, nudging his shoulder.

He curls his lip. "There's no such thing as too much ice cream, Imaan."

Olivia laughs a little. "This is true. You're so smart, buddy!"

Amir grins at her, then turns to London. "Did Candy eat too much ice cream?"

London shakes her head. "No, of course not. She's actually in great physical shape. I'm not sure why she's always so quiet. She's probably just shy."

We all inspect Candy as she lies silently in London's arms, half asleep. I want to hug Candy too, squeeze her gently to my chest and tell her to give a little bark of joy or something. But I'm not sure this is the right time.

"I think I see the problem," Dada Jee finally says. "This dog is depressed."

CHAPTER 5

Everyone turns to look at Dada Jee.

"What?" he says. "Animals can get sad too, you know."

"Seriously?" I narrow my eyes at Dada Jee because you can never tell when he's joking. "How do you know this?"

He sighs and sits back in his chair. "In Pakistan, my father had a horse named Sultan. Big, black fellow with a white diamond on his forehead. We kids were scared of him, but he and my father were best friends. They'd ride out into the fields every morning, galloping away like in the movies."

"He sounds incredible," I whisper. I can just imagine Sultan, majestic and beautiful.

"He was," Dada Jee says. "He was with my father for years and years. When my father died, Sultan stopped eating. He just . . . got so sad. It was obvious to everyone how much that horse missed my father."

"What happened to him?" London asks.

"Yes, Dada Jee, what happened?" It's Amir, his eyes round and mouth half-open. Amir loves hearing stories. And Dada Jee always tells the best stories.

"Nothing much," Dada Jee replies, sighing again. "Sultan got thin and slow. He stayed in the pasture with the other horses until his last days. I don't think he ever galloped in the fields like before."

There's a silence in the kitchen as we all digest Sultan's story. Wow. I never knew horses could get sad. "Maybe he was sick and nobody knew about it," I say timidly. I'm not sure why. I just don't like the idea of animals being sad and lonely.

Dada Jee shook his head. "We had the vet come out and look at him several times. There was nothing physically wrong. Just . . . grief, I suppose."

Mama's been listening quietly this whole time. Now she says, "It's difficult to handle things when someone you love dies. You just want to curl up and forget."

We're all quiet for a few seconds, taking all this in. Mama and Dada Jee both look gloomy now, so I know they're thinking about Baba. London and Olivia look super uncomfortable, like they want to run away from all this serious talk.

Suddenly, I start giggling. Candy's ears perk up and she turns her head to look at me.

"What's wrong with you, girl?" Dada Jee demands.

I giggle some more. It's funny, how we're all standing around looking serious, when it's Candy we should be thinking about. "Nothing," I gasp. "Just . . .

wondering . . . how we got from Candy to Sultan to Baba."

Dada Jee nods like he totally understands. "The circle of life, *jaan*. We all go through it, even the animals."

Mama pushes back her chair and stands. "Well, I must start working," she says. "Those tax forms won't fill themselves."

"So my friends can come over in the afternoon?" Dada Jee asks.

"Sure," Mama calls out as she leaves the room. "But you're still responsible for the kids."

"Bah!" Dada Jee grumbles. "How come I'm always responsible for you four?"

I giggle again. "Plus Candy," I say.

Dada Jee and Amir soon disappear upstairs to clean their bedrooms. Amir is very upset by the idea of cleaning anything, but Dada Jee convinces him with a promise of cartoons later. London, Olivia, and I go into what we call the Pet Room. It's a small space off the living room that used to hold junk, but I cleared it out and set it up for our pet clients. There's a big playpen with towels, plus animal toys scattered about.

London sets Candy on an empty section of the floor. "There you go, baby," she says.

Candy gives a little yelp, then ambles over to the only window in the room. She flops down with her head on the floor. We watch as she sighs, then closes her eyes.

"Wow, she looks tired," I say. Again, I just want to go over and cuddle her, but I stop myself. Candy is so different from other dogs I've met. She needs careful handling.

Olivia chews her lip. "Do you think Candy is like Sultan?"

I shrug. "No idea." I turn to London. "Does your

uncle know anything about Candy's previous owners?"

Olivia perks up. "That's probably it. She misses her owners. Or maybe they died, like your great-grandfather."

"Stop being so melodramatic," London says sharply. "I'm sure Candy is fine."

I walk over to Candy and squat beside her. She looks up at me and we gaze into each other's eyes for a second. Just FYI, she's got the most amazing brown eyes. I scratch behind her ears and she closes those eyes like she's in heaven.

"Wow, she never lets me do that," London breathes.

I scratch some more, and Candy puts her head on her paws.

London and Olivia come to kneel beside Candy, holding toys over her head.

"Here, girl, come play!" London says.

Candy opens an eye, yawns, then closes it again.

"Come on, Candy," Olivia shouts, tossing a toy toward the playpen. "Catch the ball."

Candy doesn't even look up.

Olivia throws up her hands. "This dog is no fun!"

I want to tell them to stop bothering Candy, but I clamp my jaw shut. They're just trying to cheer her up. I rush to get my laptop from my room, then sit cross-legged on the floor. "Let's do some research," I say. London and Olivia crowd around me. They watch as I type *my dog is sad* in the search bar. "I still can't believe depression is a thing for animals," London murmurs.

Apparently, it is. We find site after site about dogs being sad. Dada Jee was right. Animals can miss their owners so much they get all quiet and miserable. We see pictures of dogs with their heads on their paws, staring out windows. It's pretty much how Candy is sitting right now next to us.

"Oh, this is horrible," Olivia whispers. "Look at all these little doggies. Some of them look like they're crying."

My stomach hurts at the thought of any dog being so sad. Even though Must Love Pets takes care of all sorts of animals, dogs are the best. They're meant to chase after squirrels and catch sticks, bark madly at the mail carrier, and lick you until you can't breathe. They're not supposed to act like fluffy little statues.

Even if they're the most adorable statues like Candy.

I take a deep breath to calm myself. "These articles should say what we can do to make dogs feel better, right?" I start scrolling down quickly.

Olivia jabs a finger at the screen. "There!"

I start reading carefully. London grabs my notepad and a pen, and jots down notes. "This is fascinating!" she says, her eyes wide.

Basically, here's what you do if your dog is sad:

A. Give them lots of love. This probably means lots of snuggles and kisses.

B. Take them outside. I'm hoping walks in the park are in our future.

C. Do fun things. Music party, anyone?

Okay, that last part is more for us kids, but I think it will work wonders for Candy too. Suddenly, the awful feeling in my stomach has disappeared and I'm grinning. "This is great," I say. "We can make Candy happy."

"How?" Olivia asks. She's still staring at the laptop like it's her worst enemy.

"We'll make so much noise, she'll just *have* to participate."

London looks up from the notepad. "Yeah, and we'll have so much fun, she'll just *have* to have fun too!"

We all grin at one another. "Perfection," I say.

CHAPTER 6

The rest of the day passes quickly, now that we have a plan. London, Olivia, and I hang out all morning and afternoon in the Pet Room. We hope this will make Candy get used to us. We chat about school and books and teachers. Just normal things we'd usually talk about in my room, only now we're in the Pet Room with Candy.

I keep sneaking peeks at the cute little dog on the floor. She hasn't moved much since she first got here, just sighs and whimpers. Sometimes she yawns and stretches in an adorable way. I want to hug her and kiss her and pet her . . .

Yeah, not happening. I remind myself that she's feeling blue, and she needs sympathy.

I can do sympathy, right?

Right.

"How many books have you read this summer?" London asks me.

I groan. The summer reading challenge is so far from my mind right now. "Can I count *A Wrinkle in Time*?" I ask. It's my favorite book, and I've read it over and over.

She shakes her head. "Not if you haven't read it this summer."

Drat. Mrs. Levite is not going to be happy.

"What are you talking about?" Olivia asks.

I remember that Olivia hasn't officially started school. She and her family moved to California the day summer vacation began. "We have to read a bunch of books over the summer and then fill out this online log," I explain.

"I love reading," Olivia says.

"Same here," London replies. "Ooh, maybe we can read together."

"Great idea." I go to my room to get some books, plus my beanbag chair and pillows from the living room. Pretty soon, we're lying back on the floor, reading, chatting, and sharing quotes we like from our books.

Candy whimpers from her spot at the window. "Do you think we're disturbing her?" I whisper.

London thinks. "I don't think so. She looks comfy."

This is true. Candy somehow looks more alert than before. Her eyes are wide open and she's actually turned her head so she's looking straight at the three of us. "Maybe she likes us," I whisper again.

I don't know why, but it's very, very important that this little fluff ball like me. The more she looks at me with those shiny brown eyes, the more I fall in love with her. She's just precious, even in all her sadness.

Olivia sets down her book and declares, "No more reading! My eyes are getting tired."

"How about some music?" I ask, pulling up my laptop.

Soon, we've got music playing through the speakers on my laptop. Nothing loud, just a nice and upbeat tune that makes me smile.

London starts tapping her foot in time to the music. Olivia sings along, even though her voice quavers.

I cackle. "Wow, your brother has all the musical talent in the family, huh?" I tease. Jake, Olivia's teenage brother, is in a band with another neighbor of ours. They sang and performed for us at a neighborhood party a few weeks ago. It was fun, and they were pretty awesome.

Olivia, however, is not.

She throws a pillow at my head. "Meanie!"

I lean over to give her a hug. "I still love you."

She sniffs but continues to sing.

Then something pretty cool happens. Candy raises her head and lets out a yelp. It's so loud, it could almost be an actual bark.

"Aah!" I clap my hands over my mouth because I don't want to shout in happiness and ruin everything.

Olivia looks pleased. "Someone likes my singing."

I throw the pillow back at her. "Or maybe she's protesting."

London frowns thoughtfully. "None of the above," she says. "I think Candy is just enjoying being around us."

Interesting. When Dada Jee talked about his father's horse, it seemed like animals got sad when someone died. But maybe there are other reasons too.

"Does Uncle Tommy spend a lot of time with her?" I ask.

London shakes her head. "I doubt it. His job is really demanding. He hardly spends any time at home. And he often travels on the weekends too."

I feel a tug in my heart. "So poor Candy is alone all day?" I cry.

"No wonder she's depressed," Olivia adds.

I stand up and go to Candy. "Poor baby," I croon, scooping her into my arms. I'm half worried she'll scratch me or something, but she leans into me like she loves cuddling. Her little body is trembling slightly, and she's light as a feather. It just makes me want to hug her tighter, but I don't.

Patience, Imaan, I tell myself. I just give her a little kiss on top of her head.

"Aww," Olivia says, watching us.

"We're not going to leave you alone for even a

minute," I tell Candy firmly. "We're going to have so much fun together, you'll forget you were ever lonely."

The doorbell rings at four o'clock sharp. Amir rushes past the Pet Room toward the front door. "I got it!" he yells.

Dada Jee is right behind him. "Stop running, you rascal!" he grumbles. "You're supposed to wait for a grown-up to open the door."

It's too late. Amir pulls the front door open and yells again, "Hello!"

I go out into the hallway to see what's happening. London and Olivia are close behind me. There's lots of grunting and growling, and two elderly men come inside. One has tattoos and a big scowl. It's Mr. Greene, our next-door neighbor and a war veteran.

The other man is shorter, rounder, and has a smile under his big mustache. That's Mr. Bajpai, who lives one street over.

"Hello, girls," Mr. Bajpai says when he spies us. "I didn't know you three would be here or I'd have brought some of my famous chutney."

Dada Jee rolls his eyes as he shuts the front door. "First of all, it's not that famous," he says in a low voice.

"Of course it is. We always sell out at the farmers' market."

"Secondly," Dada Jee continues. "It's not your chutney, it's your wife's. She's the one who makes it."

Mr. Bajpai hangs his head. "That's true. It's all her hard work."

Mr. Greene glares at us as he heads toward the living room. "No cat attacks today, I hope?" he asks.

I grin. Not too long ago, Mr. Greene's workshop

was taken over by three rambunctious kittens we were pet sitting. Plus, a goat named Marmalade. They'd made such a mess that Mr. Greene was furious. But London, Olivia, and I had cleaned it up and fixed all his problems. "No kittens today," I assure him. "Only her."

I hold up Candy. She's been in my arms for the longest time, like she belongs there.

"What is that?" Mr. Bajpai asks as he passes us. He squints his eyes at Candy like he can't believe what he's seeing.

Dada Jee pushes him forward so they can all get to the living room. "It's a dog."

They all start talking at once, about how dogs are supposed to be loud and active, and blah, blah, blah.

"There's something wrong with that dog," Mr. Greene says, glaring at me like I'm responsible.

"For sure," Mr. Bajpai agrees.

"Let me tell you about my father's horse . . ." begins Dada Jee.

Amir jumps up and down. "Wanna see the doggy, Imaan!"

"Easy, buddy." Olivia pulls him away from me, but Amir keeps jumping. And yelling.

I gulp. Mama is *so* not going to like this noise. That's why she didn't want Dada Jee to bring his friends over. They're even louder and more annoying than us girls. And now they've got Amir all riled up.

I look at London with pleading eyes.

She nods, then takes a deep breath. "We've already had this discussion!" she says firmly. She's not yelling, but her voice is so strong that everyone stops to listen. Mr. Greene and Mr. Bajpai settle down on the couch. Dada Jee sits in his armchair.

Amir is still jumping, but at least he's quiet now.

"Candy's sad for some reason," London continues. "We think it's because she's been lonely."

"Yeah," I say. "We want to make her happy by surrounding her with people."

"But no shouting," Olivia adds with a stern look at Amir.

He giggles. "No shouting," he agrees.

London looks at everyone in turn. "So, are you all going to help?" she demands.

I try not to grin at her bravery. Dada Jee had no idea he and his friends would be pulled into our plans for Candy.

He scowls at us for a few seconds. Then he scowls at Mr. Greene and Mr. Bajpai. Finally, he nods. "Sure, we'll help," he grunts.

CHAPTER 7

Mrs. Harrison calls right before dinner and says Uncle Tommy is worried about his dog.

"Not worried enough to know she's depressed," I mutter under my breath.

"Shush!" London says as she speaks to her mom on the phone. She listens and nods, then hands the phone to Mama. "My mom wants to ask you something."

"What is she asking Mama about?" I hiss.

London rolls her eyes at me. "Uncle Tommy says he trusts me, so Candy needs to stay with me at night."

I don't like that at all. The Must Love Pets

headquarters are at my house, so all our clients stay here. That's why we have an official Pet Room. "I'm very trustworthy," I huff.

"I know that," London replies. "But *he* doesn't."

I frown. "You could tell him."

London throws up her hands. "You think I didn't? I told him we have testimonials from our clients and everything. He still wants me to be there."

I'm still confused. "Be where? You can't take Candy back home. Boots will pounce on him."

"No, silly, here."

Oh. I watch as Mama chats on the phone with Mrs. Harrison. I totally expect Mama to refuse, but I forgot that she and Mrs. Harrison are besties. Mama keeps saying "Mm-hmm" and "Of course, that make sense." When she puts down the phone, Mama just says, "London will be staying the night," and walks back to the kitchen.

My heart beats rapidly in my chest. "Seriously?" I squeal.

"Don't stay up too late," Mama calls out.

Ha! As if I'll be able to sleep with my friends around me. I turn to Olivia in excitement. "You should ask your parents too. We'll have a movie-and-popcorn night!"

Olivia pouts. "I already know I can't," she says. "My parents have gone out, and Jake's in charge of me."

"He'll let you stay here for sure," I protest. Jake is cool. He'll be fine with anything we ask.

Olivia shakes her head. "I don't want to get him in trouble."

I guess I understand. I'm the same way with Amir. I give her a hug. "Maybe next time."

"Imaan, get the plates out!" Mama calls. "Dinner's ready."

We eat chili and corn bread, which is totally yummy. Then we clean up the kitchen while Mama drags Amir away for his bath. He's shouting something about cartoons, but Mama ignores him.

Olivia leaves soon after that. Then it's only me and London. And Candy, of course.

Cool but also a little weird, right?

Right.

Here's why: I've never been allowed a sleepover until the first week of summer break this year. That's when we lost—and found—our first pet-sitting client, Sir Teddy. Our parents thought we deserved a reward for finding him, and let London and Olivia stay the night at my place. It was an awesome night filled with movies, pizza, nail polish, and, of course, music.

Tonight's going to be very different. But that's okay too. A sleepover is loads of fun, no matter what.

London and I quickly get ready for bed. We change into pajamas and brush our teeth, then jump under the covers. My bed is big enough for two people, which is great because I don't want my bestie on a sleeping bag on the floor.

I put a blanket on the bed near my feet and place Candy on it. She sniffs around a little, then turns a few times before flopping down on it. She gives a little yawn, and I can see her perfect little teeth. She's getting sleepy.

"Your mom will freak out if she sees that dog on the bed," London warns.

I grin at her. Candy is in the perfect place right now, and there's no way I'm moving her. "If anyone knocks on the door, I'll grab Candy and run into the closet."

Candy opens one eye and looks at me. I grin at her too. It's like she has a direct connection to my heart. "You know I'm talking about you, don't you, girl?"

"Sheesh," London says. "Of course, she knows. She's sad, not hard of hearing."

My grin fades as I think about Candy's sadness. "I

wish she could talk," I say. "I want to ask her so many questions."

"Like what?"

"I don't know," I say. "Like why she's feeling blue. Like what's her favorite thing to do. Does she like ice cream? Does she like me?"

London turns her head toward me. "You really like her, huh?"

I reach over and stroke Candy's head. "She's definitely cuteness overload," I say. "But that's not the only thing . . . It's like she actually needs me."

"Us."

"Yeah, us," I agree. "Candy needs us to help her. She needs us to take care of her and make her feel better."

"She's our mission, huh?"

I guess. I know London thinks it's a Must Love Pets thing, but honestly, it's more than that. It's an Imaan Bashir thing. I know what it's like to feel sad because

I'm missing someone. I know how Mama and Dada Jee feel without Baba. But we're all better at hiding it than Candy.

I want us all to get over Baba's dying. And since I don't know how to do that, I can at least help this adorable little dog get over whatever's bothering her.

Easy, right?

Sigh. Not really. I keep petting Candy's soft head, then her perky little ears. "I just wish I knew what to do."

"Your Dada Jee and his friends had some good ideas," London says wryly.

She's talking about Candy, of course. *No need to be so serious, Imaan,* I tell myself. I roll my eyes at London. "Eh, we'll see."

Actually, Dada Jee and Co. had hundreds of ideas, all of them hilarious. They said they could build an obstacle course in the backyard. Or they could take Candy on a road trip to New York City in Mr. Bajpai's van. Dada Jee thought they should take her cycling along the river, only I'm pretty sure none of them have ridden a bike in years. They laughed and told us stories about their childhood pets. Mr. Bajpai had a smartphone, so he read aloud articles about dogs. Mr. Greene told us all about movies with animals.

Lassie was everyone's favorite, apparently.

They also drank lots of Dada Jee's lemonade. Straight from the lemon trees in our backyard, it's the most delicious thing you ever tasted, especially in the summer.

I thought the three guys were so cute. Best friends, just like London, Olivia, and me.

Also, like Mama and Mrs. Harrison.

Which reminds me of something else. "Change of subject," I tell London quickly, flopping back down on my pillow.

She snorts and follows me. "What now?" We've

been friends for so long, she knows how quickly my mind jumps from one thing to the next.

"Ever notice how busy and stressed-out our moms are?"

"Uh, yeah!" London says this like we're talking about the heat in California or the blue color of the sky.

"We should convince them to take a break," I say. "They deserve a break."

London's eyes grow big. "Ooh, a spa weekend! My mom's always saying she needs one but never has time."

"Perfection!" I say. "They can go together."

London shakes her head. "They'll never agree. They'll just keep putting it off for later."

Yeah, that sounds just like Mama. "Not if we force them. Like, make the entire plan for them, with tickets and everything."

"Not sure spas have tickets."

I wave my hand. "Reservations or whatever. We can call and find out."

London is quiet for a minute. "Hmm, that might work. I can search online and see what's close to town."

"And we should include Olivia's mom too," I add.

"Really?" London wrinkles her nose. "Do you think they're friends? Mrs. Gordon is new here."

I shrug. "So what? Olivia's new and she's already our best friend."

"That's true." London thinks some more. That's what I like about her. She thinks through everything before deciding. It's the opposite of me, who likes to jump into every situation without a single worry. It's why we're such good friends—we balance each other.

"Okay," London finally says. "Let's do it."

"Yay!" I sit up again and scoop Candy into my arms. "Did you hear that, girl? Our moms are gonna go have some fun!"

Then you won't guess what happens. Candy licks my hand.

I want to shout with joy, but I just whisper "cuteness overload" and cuddle her like she's the most precious thing in the world.

CHAPTER 8

I open my eyes the next morning to find a wet thing in my face. "Ew," I groan. "Stop!"

More wetness, right on my cheek. "What *is* that?"

I hear panting. The next second, like a lightning bolt, I'm completely awake.

It's Candy. She's licking my face.

For any other dog, this would be totally normal. Slobbering is part of a dog's DNA, am I right? But with shy little Candy, every yelp and every lick are like a treasure you didn't expect to find.

I open my eyes and have to stop myself from

grabbing her. She's standing right next to my chest, peering into my face.

Which she just licked. Again.

Gross but also very awesome. I grin. "You hungry, girl?"

She looks at me with her bright eyes. Of course, she's hungry. She hardly ate anything yesterday.

"Bathroom first," London mumbles from the other side of the bed.

Oh yeah. Animals need the bathroom, just like humans. I used to be totally grossed out about pooping and peeing, but pet sitting a bunch of animals has made me sort of an expert.

I slip out of bed and scoop Candy in my arms. It feels so right that I stand still for a moment just to soak it in. Then we go downstairs together. It's quiet, so I check the clock in the hallway. Seven thirty-five. Mama will be up soon.

"You wake up early, huh, girl?" I whisper to Candy.

She just pants in my arms. Okay, then. Not really a morning person.

I let myself out into the backyard and set Candy down. She walks slowly to the bushes, sniffing things suspiciously. I shake my head. We took her out to the backyard to do her business twice yesterday. She should be used to this place by now.

She sets out toward the back of the yard. When I see her direction, I jump into action. "Hey, not Dada Jee's lemon trees!"

I take a hold of her collar and guide her toward some other bushes. Once she's done, I start bending to pick her up. But then I change my mind. Surely, she doesn't need to be carried everywhere?

"C'mon, girl!" I call out, backing away. I clap my hands to get her attention. "Let's go back inside and eat some breakfast."

She perks her ears at the mention of breakfast. Then . . . another miracle. She runs toward me.

Well, actually she walks, but it's a pretty fast walk, with mouth open and tongue hanging out. She's got tiny legs, so she takes a while to get to the back door. But I stay with her, and when we get inside, I say, "Good job, Candy!" like she's won a race or something.

She yelps a little to show me she's happy.

In the kitchen, Candy explores under the table while I get her food. She doesn't seem too interested in breakfast anymore, so I drag her out and offer her the bowl. She stares at it for a second, then takes a dainty bite.

I breathe a sigh of relief. This dog is active and eating something? That's a sign of not being sad. Even if it takes her forever to finish her food.

By the time Candy's bowl is licked clean, everyone else is downstairs for breakfast. "You girls had a good night?" Mama asks, yawning.

London nods. She's already changed into jeans and a T-shirt while I'm still in my baggy pajamas. "It was the best, Mrs. Bashir," she replies, smiling.

I smile back. "Yup."

"I'm glad to hear it," Mama says, turning to the fridge. "Parathas okay?"

London nods again, faster this time. I love how she enjoys Pakistani food as much as I do. "Ooh, yes please! I've been wanting to eat those again."

"With eggs?" I ask eagerly.

"Wouldn't have it any other way." Mama starts on the parathas. London and I sit on the floor with Candy, petting her. I expect Mama to scold us or maybe order us to take Candy outside. But she doesn't even look in our direction.

Maybe she's finally okay with Must Love Pets. That would be super awesome.

"Wash your hands before eating, Imaan and

London," Mama warns without turning around. "We don't want dog germs in our food."

So maybe not completely okay. But it's a start.

It helps that Candy isn't a wild and rowdy dog, like Sir Teddy was. It also helps that Amir isn't sneezing or sniffling with allergies. That really worries Mama.

Right now, Amir is sitting at the table next to us. He's swinging his legs while he plays a game on Mama's tablet. "Look, Imaan," he practically yells. "Watch me play."

Candy looks up at his voice. I'm worried that she'll get scared, because Amir with headphones on can be really loud. But she just gives a low bark, like she's saying something in reply.

I beam at her.

"We'll watch later," London promises Amir.

He shrugs and goes back to his game. I smile a little because Dada Jee would be so annoyed to see him playing at the kitchen table. It's a good thing my grandfather isn't up yet.

"You better put that away before Dada Jee comes in," I say.

Amir acts like he didn't hear me. I kick his leg with my foot.

"OW!" he yells. "Mama, Imaan kicked me."

I soothe his leg with my hand. "Don't be silly, it's fine now."

Mama turns to give me a warning look but doesn't say anything. *Sorry*, I mouth, grinning at her. It's such a good morning, with my bestie with me, and a cute little dog that's stealing a bit of my heart every second. Even Amir's yells and Mama's angry looks can't bring me down.

I pet Candy some more. London leans over to me. "You notice Candy's behavior?"

"Yes!" I gush. "She's more active, right?"

"Mm-hmm. I wonder why, though."

"Isn't it obvious?" I reply. "She was lonely before. Now she's surrounded by people. Kids especially. She loves it!"

London doesn't look convinced. "Really? You don't think it's too loud?"

I stroke Candy's head, and she looks up at me with her bright eyes. "You're loving all the noise around here, aren't you, Candy baby?"

She licks my hand. I beam again.

When the parathas are almost done, someone rings the doorbell. A minute later, Dada Jee shuffles in with Olivia behind him. She's got her camera around her neck like a real professional. "Look who I found on the front porch," Dada Jee grumbles.

"Good morning, everyone!" Olivia says chirpily.

"Come in." Mama smiles. "You're just in time for parathas."

"What are those?"

"Only the most delicious bread in the world," London replies, dragging her over to the table.

I wash my hands at the sink, then nudge London to do the same. She rolls her eyes but obeys. Nobody wants to get on Mama's bad side.

The three of us sit down side by side, Candy at our feet. Dada Jee sits down too. His foot is right next to Candy, and she shifts a little so she's half lying on top of it. My eyes widen in alarm, waiting for Dada Jee to freak out like he did every time Sir Teddy came too close. But he does the complete opposite. He leans down and whispers. "You're a quiet one, eh?" he says.

She yawns, then settles even more firmly on his foot. Dada Jee shakes his head and smiles a little. Then he straightens up and says, "She's cute."

Okayyy. That was definitely very un–Dada Jee–like.

Mama sits down across from me. I remove Amir's

tablet and headphones, and we dig in. London's making sounds like she's in heaven. Olivia's chewing slowly. "OMG, this is amazing!" she mumbles. "I already ate breakfast, but I could eat this all day."

"Don't talk with your mouth full," Amir tells her with a grin. Only he's also doing the same thing, and pieces of egg fly around everywhere.

"Ew, Amir, close your mouth!" I say loudly.

"You close your mouth!"

"You kids!" Dada Jee grunts. "You'll never let me eat in peace. In my day, everyone was quiet at the dining table."

"Your day, Dada Jee?" I tease. "You mean the time of the dinosaurs?"

Dada Jee scowls. "How old do you think I am, Imaan?"

"Wellll . . ."

Amir starts laughing. Then London and Olivia

start laughing too. Soon, we're all practically howling. Even Mama smiles at us as she pours tea into a cup and adds some sugar.

And then a very unusual sound reaches my ears. A full bark, high and excited. *Woof-woof-woof.*

We all turn to stare at Candy. She's standing near her bowl, tail wagging. Actually, her entire body is wagging, like a little vibrating fluff ball. She looks . . . happy. Olivia quickly takes some pictures. *Click-click!*

I want to hug Candy. I want to crush her to my chest and whisper, "Good dog!" But I only smile proudly and say, "She's happy today," like it's perfectly normal.

Because it *is* normal. Sometimes we're lonely and sad. But then other people gather around us and make us happy. I love that so much.

I want that for Candy, but I also want that for my family.

CHAPTER 9

London and I give Olivia an update on Candy after breakfast. She's trying to smile, but I can tell she's feeling bad about our sleepover.

"Don't worry, we didn't watch a movie without you," I say, rubbing her arm.

She moves her arm away. "I don't care if you did."

Ooh, she's definitely feeling bad. I bite my lip. I'm not sure what else I can do.

London asks, "Can you stay tonight?"

Wait, what? "Another sleepover?" I gasp. This is too good to be true.

London shrugs like it's no big deal. "Candy's with us for another two nights. I'm sure our moms will agree."

Olivia is smiling now. "I can stay tonight," she agrees. "I already asked my mom."

I gulp because I'm thinking of what Mama will say to all this. She's been patient with Candy so far, but I think that's because the dog is so quiet Mama forgets she even exists. That will definitely change if Candy starts barking more, like she did at breakfast.

"Where is Candy?" London asks, like she can read minds.

We're in the Pet Room, sitting on the floor like usual. My butt is getting sore with all this floor sitting. "I should bring some cushions in here," I mutter to myself.

London gives me a strange look. "Where's Candy?" she repeats.

I spy Candy behind a potted plant. She's got that sad face again, her head flopped on her paws, her eyes half closed. "Poor baby," I sigh, pointing her out to London and Olivia.

London thinks for a minute. "I know what will cheer her up!" She opens my laptop and puts on some music. Loud music.

"London!" I cry. "Mama's working!"

"Oops, sorry." She lowers the volume a little bit. Then she stands up and pulls me with her. "Come on, we're having a dance party."

Olivia jumps up too. "Ooh, great idea!"

They both start moving with the music. I don't. I have three reasons:

> A. I've never really danced to actual music before. It seems . . . extra.
>
> B. I'm sure I'm going to look awkward and weird if I try.
>
> C. I'll get in trouble with Dada Jee or Mama if they see.

Okay, I'm not 100 percent sure about the last one, but it makes sense to me. My family's from Pakistan. We do things differently. I've never seen Mama listen to music, let alone dance to it. And Dada Jee is so old-fashioned, he's always complaining about Americans and their taste in music.

It's too late to say no, though. London grabs my right hand, and Olivia grabs my left one. "Don't worry, be as silly as you like!" Olivia tells me.

That part won't be difficult, at least. Soon, we're jumping around, waving our arms and bodies like those inflatable tube guys outside stores. I giggle, which turns into a laugh. Before I know it, we're all laughing and dancing.

"This is wild!" I gasp.

"Totally," Olivia gasps back.

"But so fun, right?" London says smugly.

I sneak a peek at Candy behind the potted plant.

She's still in the same position, but now her eyes are open, and they're staring straight at us. "Candy . . . thinks . . . we're bananas!" I say breathlessly.

"She likes it," London replies. "She knows we're fun."

Olivia stops to take some more pictures of Candy. She's busy clicking when there's a knock at the door. "What're you guys doing?" comes a suspicious voice.

It's Amir. He comes all the way inside and stands with his hands on his hips like he's Mama. "Dada Jee went to the farmers' market, so you're in charge of me," he says like he's telling me a big secret.

I stop waving my arms around, but I'm still dancing (sort of). "We're having a dance party. Wanna join us?"

"Yes!" He grins and steps into our circle. The next second, he's dancing.

Like, really dancing.

London, Olivia, and I gape at him. He's only six years old, but he's got moves. He claps his hands in time with the music. He stretches out his legs and waves them around. He points his fingers in the air, then brings them back to his body. He twirls and twirls.

We all stop dancing to watch him. "Where did you learn to do that?" I choke out.

He grins again. "The internet."

After another minute, Olivia suddenly gasps, "OMG, he's doing the hokey pokey!"

She's right. Now that I know this, I can see the moves of the classic kids' dance. Amir is a pro at it. He acts like he's Justin Bieber or something. I get energized just watching him. Hey, there's no way my kid brother will be better at this than me.

I start copying his moves, and pretty soon, we're all dancing the hokey pokey like we're pros.

Well, obviously Amir is the best, but the three of us are close seconds.

When the music ends, I literally collapse on the

floor. The others follow me. "I'm the king of hokey pokey!" Amir announces, panting loudly.

"You really are!" Olivia says, fanning herself with her hands.

I drag myself up to get some water bottles for everyone. If Amir gets dehydrated on my watch, Mama will be so mad. We're sprawled on the Pet Room floor, guzzling water when I feel a wet nose on my foot.

Candy.

I smile so big my face stretches. "Did you like our performance, girl?" I whisper as I pet her.

She licks me again. I guess that's a yes.

Dada Jee returns in the late afternoon with his friends. They're holding boxes full of stuff I can't really see. "What's all this?" I ask.

Dada Jee jerks his chin toward the backyard. "Come outside and see."

We all follow him. Mr. Bajpai and Mr. Greene are already setting the boxes in the yard. "What's going on?" London asks.

"Patience, child," Dada Jee grunts.

London, Olivia, and I sit on chairs on the patio and watch patiently. Amir starts kicking around his soccer ball. He's still tired after the dance party, but I made him take a nap after lunch, so his energy is almost back to normal.

That means hyper energetic, in case anyone wants to know.

Candy sits on London's lap. I want to take her, but I remind myself she's London's uncle's dog. That makes her . . . London's cousin?

Ugh, that sounds gross.

Still, I want Candy all to myself. Since that's not

happening, I focus on Dada Jee and his besties. They're so funny. They're trudging around the backyard, pipes and wooden pieces in their hands. They keep arguing about what goes where, like one of those Three Stooges movies from the black-and-white era.

"They're so adorable," Olivia whispers to me.

"Have you seen *The Three Stooges*?" I whisper back. When she shakes her head, I say, "We'll watch it tonight on the computer."

"What are you guys building?" London calls out.

"A doggy playground," Dada Jee replies. "For Candy."

Okay, first of all, I had no idea Dada Jee knew the dog's name.

Second of all, a doggy playground? Like in dog shows? "We can't even get Candy to run around the yard," I protest. "What makes you think she'll do jumps and things?"

"The guys at the farmers' market were talking about it," Mr. Bajpai explains. "Seems like lots of dogs get depressed."

"They shared some ideas of what we can do," Mr. Greene added in his gruff voice.

"We?" London asks.

"Yes, we," Dada Jee says. "We're all going to work together to make this dog happy again."

The other two men grunt in agreement.

My heart melts at this declaration, and I jump up. "I want to help!"

"Me too!" Amir shouts.

Dada Jee grumbles under his breath, but he hands out supplies from his box. "Okay, then. You girls get to work. I'm going to fetch some lemonade for everyone."

CHAPTER 10

It's sleepover night number two, which should make me feel top of the entire world. Ready to PARTY!

Right?

Wrong. After all the dancing and playground building, I can hardly move. My muscles are sore, and my eyelids are heavy.

Great! I'm Imaan the Exhausted. Too tired to have fun at her very rare sleepover.

Still, I'm with my best friends, which is awesome. After dinner, London, Olivia, and I lie on our stomachs on my bed and watch funny videos on my laptop. I try to stay awake, but I'm yawning so big all my teeth are probably on display.

London and Olivia yawn even bigger than me.

"Maybe we should turn in," I say quietly when the first video ends.

"Good idea," Olivia replies. She and London crawl into their sleeping bags, and I put away my laptop. Candy settles down at the foot of the bed with me like before. Maybe it's just my imagination, but she seems more friendly. Her eyes are brighter. And she watched us all build the doggy playground in the backyard without falling asleep even once.

"You'll love the place when it's done," I tell her softly.

"Your Dada Jee and his friends are really going overboard," Olivia says.

"You just think that because you don't know her Dada Jee," London replies dryly. "He's a force of nature."

"Yeah, like a grumpy bear," I joke.

Turns out, Dada Jee is a hardworking bear. When we go downstairs the next morning, we see him in the backyard with Amir, putting up the last of the play structure. We stare at the sight in front of us in silence.

This thing is huge. There are steps leading up to a platform. There's a tunnel. There's a big hoop with flags all around it. There's a pit with colorful balls. Lots of balls.

"Whoa!" Olivia says. She runs back up the stairs.

"Where are you going?" I yell without turning my head. My eyes are drawn to the doggy playground like magnets.

"To get my camera!" she yells back.

Amir sees us through the window and waves. "Look, Imaan! Isn't it stupendous?"

I open the back door and we troop outside to the patio. Candy stands in the doorway. Her tail twitches like it wants to wag but has forgotten how to. She's looking right at the doggy playground with huge, bright eyes.

Olivia comes back with her camera and walks around the structure, snapping pictures from all angles. London follows her, with Amir on their heels. He wants to explain everything since he's been helping Dada Jee. He chatters nonstop and laughs a lot.

I stay next to Candy, wondering what she's thinking of all this. Finally, I nudge her with my leg. "Go on, girl. It's for you."

Dada Jee looks up. "Don't push her. She'll come in her own time."

There's a rap on the window. "Breakfast, everyone!" It's Mama. When she spies the playground, she comes outside, hands on hips.

"Who did all this?" she asks, stunned.

I grin. "Dada Jee and his friends!" Then I turn to Dada Jee. "Where are they, by the way? They should see this!"

He grunts. "They'll be here later. Bajpai has a surprise for Candy."

"What, more than this?" Mama waves her arms around. She's still in shock, I think, because her face is blank.

"You don't like it?" I whisper. I'm not sure why, but it's important to me that Mama likes the playground. And Candy.

"It's removable," Dada Jee adds quickly. "I can pick these things up anytime."

"See?" I tell Mama. "No problem!"

Mama shakes her head. "I like it. I'm just . . . shocked. You do know Candy is going back to her home tomorrow, right?"

There's silence. Even Amir stops laughing. "I know,"

I say loudly. Do I sound mad? I don't know.

Dada Jee doesn't seem concerned. "It's fine. These girls always have some animal here. They can all enjoy the playground."

"A Must Love Pets playground!" London cheers.

"Can I play in the doggy playground?" Amir shouts, jumping. "Please? Pretty please?"

"Ugh, Amir, you're scaring Candy!" I tell him. But when I look down, Candy is standing still, staring like she's in a trance.

"I think she likes it," Olivia says in surprise.

Amir is still jumping. "Can I?" he asks again. His voice is lower but whinier. I can predict a tantrum is not far behind.

Dada Jee is on it, though. He ruffles Amir's hair. "I'll think about it if you eat all your breakfast."

"Then what are we waiting for?" Amir runs indoors, and we all follow.

All except Candy, who stays on the patio, staring at the giant, colorful thing my grandfather built for her.

We finish breakfast in record time, then clean up. Usually it's just me, but today everyone helps. London and Olivia load the dishwasher. Dada Jee wipes down the table and counters. I vacuum the crumbs from the floor.

"Candy's waiting for us," Amir says as he gobbles up the last of his French toast. It's his way of cleaning up: eating all the remains.

He's an adorable genius.

Mama smiles to see everyone's excitement. "That dog is good for you all," she says.

I swallow. I keep thinking about what she said earlier, about how Candy will go home tomorrow. "I guess," I say slowly.

She rubs my shoulder. "Thank you for helping me, *jaan*. Work has been brutal these days."

"You should . . ."

She walks away, saying, "Yes, yes, take a break, I know!"

Finally, we all troop outside again. Candy is lying on the patio now, head on her paws. But she's not asleep. She looks at all of us, especially at Amir as he rushes toward the doggy playground at top speed. "C'mon, Candy!" he shouts as he jumps into the ball pit.

I still can't believe there's a ball pit in our backyard.

Candy stands up and wags her tail very slowly. But she doesn't move. It's like she's scared or something. I pick her up and take her closer. "See, baby, this is for you!" I whisper in her ear.

She barks once, like she's saying *Yes, I see that*.

"Put her down, Imaan!" London says.

I set Candy down gently on a wooden platform. She waits, then takes a step. "Yay!" I whisper-shout.

She stops and sits down on the platform.

I sigh. Baby steps, I remind myself. I think of Baba and what he'd say to me when I'd want to rush through the park, dragging him along. *Have patience, Imaan. There's no need to hurry to have fun. Take your time and enjoy every little thing.*

Amir jogs up to Candy and lies down on the platform next to her. "Careful, Amir," I say. "You don't want to get allergies again."

He ignores me. He pushes his face close to Candy's and says, "Play with me, Candy. Please?"

Candy licks his face.

I scowl. "Traitor," I say to Candy. But I'm only a little jealous. Mostly I'm happy because Candy is getting comfortable with us.

Amir gets up again and runs up and down the

platform. "Come on, Candy, come on!" he says every time he reaches her.

I'm just about to tell him to stop, when Candy gets up and barks. Not once, but twice. Then she follows Amir as he heads up the platform toward the hoop. "Good girl," he calls out. "Let's play!"

I stare after them. Amir has slowed down until he and Candy are walking side by side. He's showing her the hoop and talking to her in his loud, adorable voice. She's watching him like she understands everything.

London and Olivia come to stand right next to me. "Unbelievable," London murmurs. "It's like she's coming out of her shell."

Dada Jee grunts from behind us. "You're welcome."

CHAPTER 11

Candy gets tired after a little while, so she comes back to me. I rub her ears and she flops at my feet as I sit on a patio chair with London and Olivia. We've got my laptop with the music on low, and we're watching Dada Jee as he tends to his precious lemon trees.

"Tell us another story, Dada Jee," Olivia says.

"About what?" he asks, turning to us.

"Anything," she answers.

"Ooh, I know!" London says. "Imaan's dad."

Dada Jee is lost in his thoughts so long, I wonder if he forgot what London said. Then he clears his throat and begins. "He loved animals too, you know. He'd come home from school sometimes with an injured bird in his hands. He'd keep it in a little box lined with towels, and dig up worms from the back garden to feed it."

"Ew," I say, but I have a warm feeling in my heart to know Baba did that. Gross but amazing.

"I thought the same thing the first time I found him with one of those worms," Dada Jee tells us. "We got used to it after that."

"What else?" I ask eagerly. I can't get enough of these stories.

"Oh, lots of animals over the years. He named each one of them, even if they stayed with him only a day or two."

"Names like what?" Olivia asks. She's also enjoying the stories, I guess.

Dada Jee taps his chin. "Urdu names, mostly. But

also sometimes English names, like the ones he knew from television." His eyes light up. "Oh, you girls will like this. When Imaan's baba was in high school, he found a stray cat that was hurt. It had been in a fight or something. Blood on its face and scratches on its stomach. He cleaned him up and named him Rambo."

Olivia giggles.

I wrinkle my nose. "What's that?"

"It's a movie from the eighties," London says. "Rambo was a fighter."

Dada Jee's smile fades. He ducks his head and goes back to his lemon trees. "So was Imaan's baba."

I know he's thinking about Baba's fight with cancer. London reaches over and squeezes my hand. Olivia smiles at me. I smile back. No matter what happens, I always love hearing Baba's childhood stories. It makes me feel so close to him, like the stories envelop me in a hug or something.

Cheesy, right?

Right.

There's a noise from the door in the fence. It swings open, and Mr. Bajpai walks in with a little boy Amir's age. "Hello, hello!"

Dada Jee looks up. "Ah, I was wondering when you'd arrive," he says.

Mr. Bajpai looks around the yard. "The playground looks great!"

Dada Jee stands up, grunting. "No thanks to you and Greene."

Mr. Bajpai looks offended. He holds up a big, plastic box. It's rectangular, with holes all over. And orange. "I was busy. But look what I brought."

I think he's talking about the little boy. "You mean your grandson Rahul?"

We've met Rahul before, of course. He's six, like Amir, and also into superheroes. "Hi," he says shyly.

"Rahul! Rahul! Come see what we made!" Amir rushes over like a whirlwind and drags Rahul away to the playground.

Mr. Bajpai sets down his orange box. "I meant this. It's a surprise for your sad little dog."

London, Olivia, and I get up from our chairs and crowd around the box. "What is it?" I ask impatiently.

He opens the top of the box, and I gasp.

We all gasp, including Dada Jee. Okay, he grunts, but it's a very surprised grunt.

"No way!" Olivia whispers.

"Yes way," Mr. Bajpai says, grinning widely. Inside the box are three baby chicks, all yellow feathers and spindly legs. They're the cutest things I have ever seen, like literally.

I squeal and reach my hands into the box. "Can we pick them up?" I ask, even though I've already got one in my hand.

"Sure," Mr. Bajpai says. "But they're not for you. They're for your dog."

Olivia picks up the second one, and London takes the third. "What do you mean, they're for Candy?" I ask.

Dada Jee is already leading us to where Candy sits on the platform. "She needs some animal friends," he says, waving a hand at me.

"Aren't we enough?" I joke, waving to London, Olivia, and myself.

"No!" Dada Jee and Mr. Bajpai say together.

How rude.

Dada Jee gives me a glare, so I put the baby chick I'm holding next to Candy. London and Olivia do the same with theirs. The chicks waddle around Candy, cheeping away like they're trying to talk.

"OMG, they're absolutely adorable!" Olivia whispers. She starts clicking her camera like she's on a mission. "Just adorable."

I watch Candy, ready to steal her away if things get too overwhelming. The playground, the chicks, the two hyper boys running around pretending to be trains or something. It could be too much for a shy, lonely little dog like Candy.

But Candy doesn't seem overwhelmed.

I mean, she's still shy. She keeps her barking to a minimum, only yelping at the chicks when one gets too close to her face. Otherwise, she seems . . . happy. Her tongue is lolling out, and she's wagging her tail a little. "She loves the baby chicks," London remarks.

I sigh because it's true. "They love her too," I admit.

We watch Candy with her new friends for a while. "It's like animal playtime TV over here," London says.

"Yeah, I was totally not expecting this," I agree. "Where did the chicks even come from?"

Rahul runs up, arms outstretched. "They're *my*

chicks," he announces. "We got them from the farmers' market yesterday."

"That explains it," I mutter. I've been to the farmers' market once. It's a very cool place, with food and rides. Plus, farm animals.

"These baby chicks are the cutest!" Olivia says.

Rahul shrugs. "They're gonna grow up to be superhero chickens."

That sounds scary, but I don't say anything. I just give my best eye roll.

"I want superhero chickens too!" Amir yells from the platform. Candy gives a little bark like she agrees with this plan.

"Kids," Dada Jee and Mr. Bajpai grumble together.

"Thank you for sharing your baby chicks with Candy," I say to Rahul with a grin.

"You're welcome!" Rahul grins back, then runs off again.

I put the music back on, volume higher than usual. Dada Jee and Mr. Bajpai get the patio chairs, so London, Olivia, and I sit on the ground. Amir and Rahul yell and run around, acting like wild animals.

I'm just glad Amir has someone to play with. A couple of times I worry they'll step on Candy or the chicks, but they stay away from that part of the playground. Everyone's having too much fun to notice when things get really loud.

Mama comes outside with a big frown on her face. "I can hear you all the way inside!" she practically shouts over us.

Oops. I lean over to stop the music. London pulls Amir to her as he runs past, and Olivia does the same to Rahul.

"Apologies, Amna," Dada Jee says quietly. "Go back to work."

Mama is too upset to listen. "I was on a phone call

and had to hang up because I couldn't hear myself think!"

I jump up from the ground. "Mama, don't stress. We'll leave, okay?"

She pauses to glare at me. "What?"

"We can go to the park," London says quickly. "Right, Imaan?"

I nod. London and Olivia nod. They nudge the boys, so the boys nod too. We all turn to Dada Jee. He stares back like he has no idea what's going on. "We'll go to Greene's and play some cards," he finally says, grabbing his cane. "He wants some more lemonade anyway."

"Good." Mama relaxes and turns to go. Then she twirls around with another fiery glare. Her voice quivers with anger. "Imaan, are those chickens in my yard?"

CHAPTER 12

The baby chicks turn out to be a problem. Mama doesn't want them to stay in our backyard unsupervised. Mr. Bajpai doesn't want to lug around their big orange box. Rahul thinks they'll transform into superhero chickens any second, so he wants to stay close to them.

Candy's the biggest problem, though. She refuses to leave them.

When I snap my fingers and say, "C'mon, girl," she doesn't even look at me. Even when I say "walk" and "park" and "fun" in an excited tone, she just ignores me.

Rude.

It's not her fault, though. Baby chick number one is standing on top of Candy's head, pecking at her ear. Baby chicks number two and three are nuzzling at her side like she's their mama. Candy looks like she's absolutely loving all the attention.

I want to give her a high five.

I also want to drag her out of here. "We need to leave," I say nervously. Mama's gone back inside, but I know she'll be back if she sees we're still here. "What should we do, guys?"

"Stop being so dramatic, Imaan," London says. She picks up the chicks one by one and puts them back in their box. They cheep like they're offended. "You can come with us too," she tells them, sighing.

I'm not sure it's a good idea to bring baby animals of any kind into a park. But we really don't have a choice. I fetch Candy's leash from the Pet Room and put it around her. When I pull her gently, she starts to walk with me.

"You could carry her," Olivia suggests.

I don't want to. I think it's good for her to walk. She's been treated like a sad little doggy for too long. "It's fine," I say. "She can walk, can't you, girl?"

Now that her new best friends are locked up in their orange box, Candy remembers what *walk* means. She gives a little yelp.

Olivia laughs. "I guess that means yes!"

We leave my house in a line. I'm in the front with Candy. Behind me is London and the orange box of baby chicks. At the end is Olivia, holding Amir and Rahul by the hand. "We can walk by ourselves!" Amir protests.

"I know you can, buddy," Olivia soothes him. "I'll let go as soon as we get to the swings."

"I love swings," Rahul cries.

"I'm the king of swings," Amir boasts.

They rush to the swings as soon as we get inside the park. Thankfully, it's early in the morning, so it isn't too crowded. They find two empty swings side by side and climb on like monkeys. "Stay close!" I yell.

Amir waves back. I try not to shudder at the way he's bending backward on the seat, his legs in the air.

Olivia snaps a picture of him and shows it to me on the LCD display. Amir's mouth is wide open with laughter, and his hair is hanging straight down. "He's having fun," she tells me.

I grunt, then I roll my eyes because I sound like Dada Jee. Taking care of Amir can make anyone feel grumpy.

London heads to our picnic table and puts the orange box on top. The chicks are cheeping loudly now. "They sound mad," I say. "I guess they want to play."

London removes the lid. "Sorry, kiddos, this is the best I can do." The walls of the box are too high for the chicks to leap over, but at least they can see the sky.

London and Olivia flop down on the picnic bench, but I keep standing. Candy is sniffing at a leaf on the ground, and I don't want to disturb her. This is the first time I've seen her take an interest in her surroundings.

"What *is* that, Candy?" I croon. "It's a leaf from a tree! Yes, it is!"

"Ugh!" London groans.

I raise my eyebrows. "What?"

"You sound like you're talking to a toddler," Olivia tells me.

"Candy's way smarter than a toddler," I reply.

They both snicker at me. I toss my hair and go back to watching Candy, aka the cutest dog in the universe.

Woof-woof!

I whirl around at the sound of a familiar loud barking. "Sir Teddy!"

A big golden retriever bounds toward me, pulling his owner by the leash. It's Mrs. Jarrett, who lives on our street. "Hello, girls," she says, smiling. "Pet sitting another one, eh?"

"Always." I pick Candy up so she doesn't get scared of Sir Teddy. He's a cutie pie, but his size might worry a little dog like Candy.

We all say hi to Mrs. Jarrett, then hug and pet Sir Teddy like we haven't seen him in years. He's super excited. His tail wags so fast it's a blur, and he barks so loud it echoes around us. *Woof-woof-woof!*

"OMG, we missed you so much!" Olivia says, rubbing Sir Teddy's head.

"When can he stay with us again, Mrs. Jarrett?" London asks.

"I'll let you know next time I'm going to visit my mother," Mrs. Jarrett replies.

Sir Teddy pushes his nose against my waist, touching Candy's legs gently. "He wants to say hello," Mrs. Jarrett tells us.

Carefully, I lower Candy until she's at eye level with the big dog. "Teddy, meet Candy," I say. "Be gentle, okay?"

He is *so* gentle. He stays completely still and sniffs Candy's face and ears and then . . . ew, her butt. She yelps a little and wags her tail.

"She's saying hello!" I whisper, delighted.

After Mrs. Jarrett and Sir Teddy leave, we go back to the picnic table to relax. I place Candy on the table with the box of chicks. She sits down right next to them, watching with bright, clever eyes. The chicks waddle over to the side closest to her, pushing against one another.

I stroke one chick on the head. It's the softest feeling, like air and feathers and warmth. "Whoever thought dogs and baby chicks would be friends?"

Olivia fiddles with her camera. "Sir Teddy was friends with a squirrel," she points out.

Ah yes, Flash. Sir Teddy's best friend.

"Remember the kittens with the goat Marmalade?" London asks. "That was really unusual too."

"And the three of us," I say.

Olivia looks up. "What do you mean?"

I shrug. It's hard to explain. I know we're not different species like our animal friends. But still. London, Olivia, and I have very different personalities. "We're nothing alike, but we're besties," I finally say.

London grins. "Because we have things in common too. Like animals. And loving our families."

"And having fun!" Olivia adds. "Lots and lots of fun."

I laugh, turning to make sure Amir and Rahul are still at the swings. I don't see them, which makes my heart miss a beat. I quickly scan the park.

The boys are squatting on the grass near the fence, poking at something with long sticks. "I hope that's not an ant hill," I mutter.

"It's just the soil from my dad's plantings," Olivia says, pointing.

Sure enough, Mr. Gordon and his crew are back

near the fence, just like a few days ago. They've got tree saplings this time, and big bags of soil stacked in a pile. "Guess they're going to plant trees or something there," London says.

"There should still be a bench, though," I whisper, remembering the one that used to be there before. Funny how I hadn't remembered sitting on that bench with Baba for such a long time. Now, though, that's all I can think of when I looked at the empty space.

The bench and Baba are both gone now, and Mr. Gordon is going to cover up that space with something else.

I stare at the scene miserably. Maybe I'm turning into Imaan the Sad, just like Candy.

London suddenly shifts next to me. "OMG!"

"What?" I ask without looking at her.

London keeps shifting, like she's not sure of what to say or do. "Um, nothing!" She turns to Olivia and whispers something in her ear. Only, it's not a small sentence or two. The whisper keeps going on and on like she's telling a story.

Olivia nods and smiles, covering her mouth with her hand.

I try not to get annoyed. "What's going on with you two?"

They straighten up quickly. "Nothing," they both say together.

I don't believe them, but it's lunchtime, and Amir and Rahul are digging into the dirt like they're looking for hidden treasure. If one of them gets bitten by ants, they'll scream the neighborhood down.

I stand up. I don't have time to think about Baba or Candy, or even what my two friends were whispering about behind my back. It's time to go home.

CHAPTER 13

Amir lets out a sneeze as soon as we enter the house. Before I can say anything, he sneezes again, then again and again. *Achoo-achoo-achoo!*

In a few minutes, he's changed completely. His nose gets red and drippy—disgusting, I know—and his eyes water. Mama looks just about ready to turn into a dragon and burn the house down. "What happened to him?" she almost yells at us. "He was fine when he left for the park!"

I shuffle my feet. "Um . . . there were ants . . ."

London elbows me. "You don't get allergies from ants," she whispers in my ear.

"How do you know it's allergies?" I demand.

Mama points at Amir's red face. "Oh, it's allergies all right!"

"But . . . it couldn't be the pets," Olivia protests. "We've had Candy for more than two days now."

"But you girls now also have chickens!" Mama laughs a little when she says this, but it's an angry laugh, like she's not actually finding anything about this situation funny.

According to Mrs. Levite, this is called sarcasm.

Amir sneezes again, then looks upset with himself. "Sorry."

Olivia rubs his back in soothing motions. "It's not your fault, buddy."

He sniffs like he's really sad. I groan. This is ridiculous. Amir had severe allergies when summer break started and we got our first pet-sitting client. Mama took him to the doctor and got him tested, but the test was inconclusive. That means nobody knows what he's allergic to in the first place.

I'm guessing it's too many cartoons, but nobody will believe me.

"Maybe I should call the doctor again," Mama says, searching for her phone.

"I'm fine!" Amir protests. "Rahul just gave me some germs or something."

Poor Rahul. We'd forgotten all about him. He crosses his arms over his chest. "Did not!"

I pat him on the head. "It's okay, this isn't your fault either."

He still doesn't look happy. He turns and stomps out the front door. "I'm going to my granddad."

"Wait!" I run after him because I don't want him crossing the street by himself. Then I remember that Mr. Bajpai is playing cards next door at Mr. Greene's house. I watch Rahul until he disappears inside Mr. Greene's house.

When I go back inside, I realize Rahul has left his three baby chicks with us.

Great.

We spend the night at Olivia's house. Amir has stopped sneezing thanks to Benadryl, and Dada Jee has come back from Mr. Greene's house to look after him.

Since Mama doesn't want any more animal influence in the house, we trudge to Olivia's for our third sleepover in a row.

This time, it doesn't seem as exciting.

Maybe it's because I got used to spending nights with my friends, so it's not a big deal anymore. Or maybe it's because I'm worried about Amir.

"Welcome to my house," Olivia says cheerfully as we enter.

I squint at her. I have no idea what she means

because London and I have been to her house so many times already. Then I see her looking at the pet carrier in my hand, and I realize she's talking to Candy.

Or she could be talking to the baby chicks in their bright orange box. London's holding that in both hands.

Candy whines. The chicks cheep.

"They're saying thank you for inviting us!" Olivia says.

I roll my eyes at her cheesiness and head inside.

Mr. and Mrs. Gordon are out, but they've left pizza warming in the oven. We pile our plates and head to Olivia's room. Jake's bedroom door is open, and I peek in. It's empty. "Where's Pixie?" I ask.

Pixie is Jake's very clever parakeet. We've taken care of her in the past, and she is ah-mazing.

Olivia shrugs. "Probably asleep."

Sure enough, Pixie's cage is in the corner of the room, covered with a blanket. That means she's in darkness, getting her beauty sleep. "Has she learned any new words lately?" I ask.

"I have no idea," Olivia replies. "Ask Jake when you see him next."

I definitely will. I love talking animals because it means they're super smart.

Once we're in Olivia's room, we close the door and let Candy and the chicks out. Candy sniffs around before settling down in the middle of the floor. The chicks decide she's an obstacle course. They run over her back and under her legs. They peck at her fur and jump from her head.

We sit around them in a circle, plates in our laps.

"This is better than TV," London remarks as she eats her pizza.

"Mm-hmm," I reply. I watch Candy shake her head and move her tail away from the chicks' sharp beaks. I try not to giggle when my mouth is full.

We're almost finished with our food when we hear the sound of the garage opening right under Olivia's room. "That's my dad!" Olivia cries, jumping up.

"Ooh," London says. She puts down her half-eaten plate and stands up too.

"Okay?" I'm not sure why this is exciting news.

They head toward the door. "We'll be right back," Olivia says. "I just want to say hi to my mom and dad. I haven't seen them all day."

I put aside my plate. "Sure, I'll come too."

"No!" London practically yells.

I stare at her.

She swallows. "No, that's okay," she says in a normal voice. "You stay with the animals."

Olivia adds, "Yeah, make sure they don't get into any trouble."

"Stay here!" London tells me. "We'll be back soon."

Then my best friends rush out of the room like their pants are on fire.

I watch the animals for twenty minutes. I know this because I'm also watching the clock in the base of Olivia's table lamp.

How could it take them twenty whole minutes to say hi to Mr. and Mrs. Gordon? And why does London need to say hi too?

I get up from the floor. Time for some answers, right? Right.

I look at the animals again. Olivia was right, someone needs to make sure they don't get in trouble. Candy is asleep, stretched out on the rug. I put the chicks back in their box. "Stay here!" I say. Then I realize that's exactly what London said to me before she left.

"Ugh," I whisper to myself.

I close the bedroom door so Candy doesn't escape if

she wakes up. Then I creep down the stairs like a thief. I hear voices from the kitchen, so that's where I go.

The kitchen is almost dark. The only light is coming from the top of the stove. I creep closer, but I don't enter. I can hear whispers and giggles.

I lean forward and blink. London and Olivia are huddled at the kitchen table. Their heads are close together, and they're talking.

It's how London and I used to talk before Olivia moved here. All secrets and giggles and nudges.

The worst part? Mr. and Mrs. Gordon are nowhere around. Which means my friends lied to me about going downstairs to greet them.

My chest hurts as I watch the scene. I take a huge breath, turn around, and walk back up the stairs with trembling legs.

I guess I'm Imaan the Pathetic. No dog. No Baba. No friends.

CHAPTER 14

"Hey, what's up?" It's Jake. He's funny, even if he's traitor Olivia's big brother. He's sitting on a chair in his room now. He's got earbuds in his ears and a phone in his hand.

"Nothing." I'm in no mood for a conversation.

He puts the phone down on his desk. "You okay?" he asks. "You sound grumpy."

I enter his room. I don't really want to go back to Olivia's room. I also don't want to go home.

"Is Pixie already asleep?" I ask, ignoring his question.

"Let's check." He gets up and goes to the cage in the corner. "It's past her bedtime, but she usually stays awake for a while."

I stand near the cage while he lifts the blanket and whistles softly. "Hey, Pixie!" he whispers.

"Hello!" comes the shrill reply.

Jake removes the blanket and opens the cage door. "Come here, you beautiful girl." He reaches in and brings Pixie out, holding her gently.

She flaps her wings when she sees me. "Hello, everyone! What fun we're going to have today!"

I laugh. "Hello to you too, Pixie!"

Jake gives me a sidelong glance. "Feeling better, I see."

"Yeah."

"Wanna talk about it?"

I sigh. Do I? I don't usually talk much with Jake, but there's nobody else right now. Pixie may be able to say words, but she can't give advice or tell me how needlessly dramatic I'm being. "London and Olivia are having fun downstairs all by themselves," I finally say. "They left me in the room alone to watch Candy and the baby chicks for twenty whole minutes."

Jake looks at me thoughtfully. It's weird, because he's usually got a smug grin on his face and is always cracking jokes. "You don't have to be with your friends all the time, you know."

I frown. "Really? The three of us do everything together."

"Maybe that's your problem."

I frown more. He's being ridiculous. "We're best friends. How is it a problem to spend all our time together?"

He shrugs. "You're not clones. You can be apart from one another and still have fun."

"Impossible!"

"Think about it," he insists. "Don't you and London do things together that don't involve my sister?"

I stroke Pixie's head as I think about this. London and I had a sleepover the other day. Did Olivia feel bad about it? Probably, but I never asked. I just assumed it was okay. "I guess," I mutter.

"So why can't she and London chat without you for twenty minutes? It's not that big a deal, right?"

"Big deal!" Pixie calls out in her shrill voice. "Big, big deal."

"You're right, Pixie," I tell her solemnly. "Twenty minutes isn't a big deal at all."

"Really?" Jake asks. "Does that mean you're okay? No more pouting?"

I scoff. I was *so* not pouting.

There's a knock at the open door. "Hey, Imaan!" It's Olivia. "What are you doing in here?"

"Nothing. I just wanted to see Pixie." I'm still

not completely happy about what I saw in the kitchen, but I understand it. Sort of. I try to smile, and my lips wobble.

"Hello!" Pixie greets them. "What fun we're going to have!"

Jake puts her back into the cage and fixes the blanket over it. "Not tonight, birdie!"

"Help! Help! Somebody call nine-one-one!" Pixie shouts.

My eyes pop. "That's new!" I say. "Did she just learn that?"

Jake looks proud. "Yup! Been working on it all week."

"Amazing."

Olivia rolls her eyes and heads to the door. "Let's go back to my room. We need to decide what movie we're watching."

London holds up a container. "Plus, we found ice cream!"

When we get back to my house in the morning after breakfast, nobody's there. *Gone to the doctor for Amir's allergies*, says a note on the kitchen counter.

I bite my lip in horror. I'd totally forgotten about Amir and his sneezathon.

"You can't do anything about it now," Olivia says, giving me a hug.

"Yeah, we have clients to take care of," adds London. She strides toward the backyard, holding the orange box.

I follow slowly, Candy's carrier in my arms. "But it doesn't make sense," I say loudly. "What's he allergic to this time?"

We bring out Candy and the chicks and place them gently on the play structure Dada Jee and his friends built. Candy barks a little. The chicks race to it, cheeping wildly.

"Go have fun!" I tell them.

London fishes a piece of paper from her jeans pocket. "I was thinking the same thing about Amir's allergies," she says.

"What's that?" I squint.

"I've made notes on all the times and places that Amir started sneezing," London reminds me. "Starting from the first day when Sir Teddy came home with us."

I remember now. She'd promised Mama she'd track the *allergy incidents* and make a report.

London is super smart, so I'm sure she'll make an amazing report.

We pore over the paper. Amir sneezed with Sir Teddy (a dog) but not Candy (also a dog). He sneezed with Marmalade (a baby goat) but not Doc (a bunny) or Clyde, Missy, and Bella (kittens). "It's so confusing," I finally groan. "If he's allergic to dogs, why not Candy until now?"

Olivia switches on her camera and starts to go through the LCD screen. "Maybe we can get some clues from my pictures."

I'm not sure what she means. Olivia's photography is incredible, but there are zero pictures of my snot-nosed brother sneezing away like a train.

Then London taps on the screen, where Amir is upside down on the swing. "Wait. It wasn't until we went back to the park that Amir got his reaction."

"And Sir Teddy is at the park, like, all the time!" Olivia quickly says.

"But not Marmalade," I reply.

Olivia clicks backward to find their pictures. Marmalade is at the farmers' market on a patch of grass and mud.

"What do these all have in common?" London says slowly, like she's talking to herself.

"Trees?" I guess. "Mud? People?"

"Ha!" Olivia rolls her eyes at my last guess. "You sound like your Dada Jee and his posse."

"Nobody says posse anymore," I protest, laughing.

"They do in Texas."

"That's a stereotype," London points out.

I hear a series of timid barks from the doggy playground and jump up. "Time to play!"

The dog-and-chick combo is already having fun. Unlike yesterday when Candy was lying around and the chickens were climbing around her, today she's much more active.

Candy is trotting on the platform, her tongue hanging out. The chicks are following her like she's their mama. "OMG, look how cute they are!" Olivia cries.

My heart soars to see Candy having fun. I pick up a plastic toy that Amir's left in the grass, and wiggle it around in front of her. "You can do better than that, Candy!"

Guess what? She can.

She increases her speed until she's practically running. I move backward so she can't catch me. The baby chicks are after us, but they're so tiny, they're soon left behind. Candy comes to a hoop and hesitates. "Come on, girl," I say. "You can do it."

"Imaan . . ." London calls out. "Maybe you should slow down."

I don't want to. I'm so happy that Candy is finally acting like a happy, well-adjusted dog. She deserves to have fun. She deserves to play and bark and make friends, even if they're from another species.

I'm still thinking this when something terrible happens.

Candy tries to jump through the hoop, but she falls short. By a lot. I guess Dada Jee and his posse weren't really thinking about dog height when they built this thing. She rolls back onto the platform, only she doesn't stay still.

She rolls a little, then comes to a stop at the edge of the platform where the wood is sticking out a little bit into a sharp point.

She yelps so loudly my ears hurt and my heart thunders.

Because Candy, the most adorable and quiet dog in the entire world, is in pain. And it's all my fault.

CHAPTER 15

I don't stop to think about it. I grab Candy and run back inside the house. London and Olivia are close behind me, asking what happened.

I ignore them. All my focus is on the doggy in my arms. "It's okay, Candy," I say. "I've got you."

She whimpers. Loudly.

I feel so bad, I don't know what to do.

But doing nothing isn't an option when an animal is hurt. I set her down on the living room floor and crouch next to her. London and Olivia kneel on either side of me.

"Give me some space, please!" I say as I inspect Candy carefully. Her head, her tummy. Her legs. Finally, I see it. Her front right paw is bleeding. It's not too bad, but she's obviously in pain.

"OMG!" Olivia breathes in a panicky voice.

"We need to get to a vet, pronto!" London almost shouts.

"Shush!" I hiss sharply.

London's already standing up. "What do you mean, shush?"

I look up at her. "We can't go to a vet. Nobody's home to take us."

She looks around like she'll find the answer to our problem on the walls or something. "My parents are at work too," she mutters. Then she stops. "Oh, Olivia's mom!"

Olivia's eyes widen. "She went to the mall. She told me before she left."

I shake my head. "It's okay. We can take care of this ourselves. It's not a big deal."

"It's definitely a big deal, Imaan!" Olivia's voice is even more panicky now. "There's blood!"

"This isn't the time for panic," I say calmly. "We're pet sitters. All this is part of the job."

"But . . ." London begins.

I interrupt her. "Candy needs us to be strong, you guys."

Olivia nods so fast, her ponytail swishes around. "You're right, of course!"

I turn to London. "Go get my laptop."

She's shocked. I'm not usually the one ordering people around.

"Please?" I add.

She nods and runs up the stairs to my room. I turn to Olivia. "There's a first aid kit in the hallway closet," I tell her. "Can you get it?"

Olivia rushes to the hallway so fast, her feet skid on the floor.

Candy whimpers again. I rub her head. "I know, baby," I say softly. "We'll fix you up in no time."

When London comes back with the laptop, I ask her to search *how to fix a dog's hurt paw*. Then I put Candy on my lap and use the first aid kit Olivia brought to do exactly what the instructions say.

Wash the wound with water. Check.

Dry the paw. Check.

Apply antibiotic cream. Check.

Bandage the wound. Check.

Hug and kiss the dog over and over. This one isn't in the instructions but still, triple check. The three of us basically create a warm wall around Candy with our arms.

"I'm so glad she's okay," Olivia whispers.

"You shouldn't have doubted me," I say, smirking.

London nudges me. "You were scared too, admit it."

I lose the smirk. "I was *so* scared!" I agree. "But Candy needed someone calm. You two did too!"

London rolls her eyes but doesn't say anything.

We're still hugging Candy—and one another—when the back door slams open. Amir rushes in, followed by Mama and Dada Jee. Candy barks happily in greeting, which is great because (a) it means she feels fine after her accident, and (b) she's no longer the shy, quiet creature she used to be a few days ago.

I hug her extra for both those reasons.

"Guess what, Imaan!" Amir yells, screeching to a halt near us.

"You got ice cream?" I guess.

His face falls. "How did you know?"

I roll my eyes. "You're holding the cone in your hand, silly."

"Oh yeah!" He offers it to me. "Want some?"

"Ew, no, thanks."

"Okay." He runs up the stairs. "I'm going to call Rahul on the phone! Dada Jee says he'll help me dial."

"Tell Rahul to come get his baby chicks!" London calls after him. "Otherwise, he has to pay us for pet-sitting services!"

I nudge London. "Good idea. Let's send Mr. Bajpai a bill or something."

London grins. Then she spies Dada Jee's scowl as he trudges slowly behind Amir. "Just kidding, Dada Jee!"

I can hear Mama fixing herself a cup of tea in the kitchen. I pet Candy while London and Olivia go back outside to collect the baby chicks. They're in their box, snoozing, when Dada Jee comes back downstairs. "Mr. Bajpai will come for the chicks in a few minutes," he tells us.

Mama comes into the living room with her tea and

sits on the couch. "What's going on here?" she asks, pointing to the first aid kit and open laptop.

"Candy got hurt," Olivia rushes to explain. "And we were so freaked out!"

"Speak for yourself," I say dryly.

"Okay, I was freaked out. And London too . . ."

"Hey!"

"But Imaan was amazing!" Olivia continues like a runaway train. "She told us exactly what to do, and we looked up the first aid instructions online, and then we cleaned and wrapped up Candy's paw, and it was so easy. I thought we'd have to go to the vet, but there was no need."

When Olivia comes to a stop, she's panting.

London pats her on the back. "Imaan was more than amazing. She didn't panic at all."

I flush because London saying that about someone else is high praise. She's the queen of calm.

Mama sits back with arms across her chest and stares at me. It's a weird look, not angry but something else. Almost like she's really seeing me for the first time. "Really, Imaan?" she asks quietly. "You figured everything out by yourself?"

I shrug. "It wasn't too hard. I've done it before with Amir many times."

Dada Jee grunts in agreement. Amir is so hyper he gets hurt all the time. If Dada Jee's not around, I'm the one who patches him up and kisses his boo-boos. Just like I did with Candy.

Come to think of it, Amir and Candy are alike in a lot of ways. I love them both to bits, but they're also a handful to take care of.

I place Candy back on the floor. "You're a good dog," I say. "You didn't freak out like Olivia!"

"This is true." Olivia laughs.

Mama's face creases into a little smile too. "I'm

proud of you, *jaan*," she says. "You've proven yourself quite responsible."

My hand freezes over Candy's head. My heart starts to thud inside my chest. "Responsible?" I ask slowly. It's the word I've been using all these months when I talk about a pet. Every time I've begged Mama for a dog, I've tried to convince her I'm *responsible* enough.

Mama nods, still smiling that mysterious smile. "Yes, responsible. I thought you couldn't take care of a pet, but you've proven me wrong. The three of you have taken care of so many animals, I'm impressed with you."

Dada Jee grunts in agreement again. I suddenly wonder if I'm dreaming right now because having both my mother and grandfather happy with me at the same time is a bit unrealistic. It almost never happens.

Then Mama says something that's basically right

from out of a dream. "The way you took care of Candy today proves that you're capable of taking care of your own dog."

There's silence as I digest this information.

Then Olivia squeals beside me. I hardly hear it over my galloping heart.

"Do you want me to pinch you?" London whispers in my ear.

"Please do," I whisper back.

She grins and pinches my arm lightly. I shake my head and come out of the daze. "Really, Mama?" I half shout, making Candy jump to her feet.

"Really," Mama replies, smiling bigger.

I jump up too and launch myself at her. "OMG OMG thank you thank you thank you!" I hug her, then turn around and hug London and Olivia, who are both jumping up and down as well. There are lots of squeals and gasps and laughter. So much laughter.

"Don't I get a hug?" Dada Jee says grumpily. "I'm the one who convinced her."

I run to him and throw my arms around him. "You did? Thank you thank you thank you!"

"Well!" Mama huffs. "It's true, your dada gave me his opinion. But I didn't make up my mind until right now when I saw how you handled the accident."

"Because I'm responsible," I say, grinning.

"Imaan the Responsible," Olivia says, and gives me a high five.

CHAPTER 16

We decide to celebrate, so we go to Tasty, of course.

It's a little café at the edge of our neighborhood, full of cool vibes and delicious food. The furniture is all red and shiny, and old-school music streams from something called a jukebox. It's one of the best places on earth, seriously. Not only because of the food or vibe, but also because animals are allowed inside.

Any place that welcomes animals is special, right? Right.

We order our favorite smoothies. Strawberry Kiwi

for me, Berry Berry Wild for London and Olivia. "No charge," Angie, the owner, says. "Since you girls are such big helpers."

"Thank you," London replies. We'd helped Angie organize the most incredible block party earlier this month. As a reward, she'd promised us free smoothies for life.

"Yeah, thanks!" I bounce on my feet, grinning. It's the same grin that's been on my face since Mama's bombshell announcement earlier today. I tried fixing my face to regular Imaan, but it's no use. Excited Imaan is here to stay for now.

"You're welcome," Angie replies, grinning back. Then she sees Candy on the floor. "A new pet today?"

Candy looks back quietly. She's still shy around strangers, but that's okay. She can't change her entire personality in one day.

Angie looks delighted. "I'll get this cutie pie a treat."

We get our drinks, then settle in the booth, slurping from straws. "Mmmm," Olivia sighs. "This is the best."

"Just what I need to celebrate my awesome news!" I say.

"I still can't believe your mom said yes!" Olivia says, sighing.

"How many times did she say no, Imaan?" London asks. "Forty-two? Forty-three?"

I shrug, trying not to think about it. "Something like that. I lost count."

Olivia giggles. "They're all so tired all the time. All the moms. She probably said yes because she's so exhausted!"

My smile slips a little. "That's true. The exhausted part anyway. We should get those spa thingies we talked about. A girls weekend. No kids. No pets."

London snaps her fingers. "Yes, let's do it!"

Angie comes over to wipe down the table next to

us. "You girls talking about a spa? I went to a really nice one last year and still have some gift certificates."

"Ooh," I say, sitting up. "Can you help us set it up? If you have time, that is."

She taps a finger on our table. "I always have time for loyal customers."

It only takes a few minutes. Angie pulls us into the back room of her café and shows us the website of a resort in Palm Springs. It's all fancy and ladylike. "Our moms will absolutely love this!" I cry, clasping hands with Olivia and London.

"I've got gift certificates for spa treatments, but you'll need to reserve a room for them," Angie says.

"Can you do that?" I ask. "I can give you all my birthday money."

London squeezes my hand. "Me too. I have my allowance."

"Me three," agrees Olivia.

Angie looks at the website again. "Hmm, not sure your allowances would be enough."

I snap my fingers. "Dada Jee would help, for sure."

"And my dad too," London adds. "He's always telling Mom she needs to take a break from work."

"Same," Olivia adds cheerfully.

"Sounds good." Angie clicks and types some more. "I'll make the reservations, and you girls can pay me back later. This weekend okay?"

"Um . . ." Olivia says, shuffling her feet. "I'm not sure . . ."

I turn to her, surprised. "What do you mean? The sooner the better, right?"

She flushes a bright red. "I guess so . . ."

What on earth is going on with her? "Is your mom busy this weekend?" I ask.

"Er . . . no."

"Then what's the problem?"

Olivia and London exchange looks. Then London says firmly: "We don't know what any of the moms have planned. We shouldn't assume."

I know Mama has nothing planned. She never does anything for herself, especially on the weekends. I frown at London and Olivia. They're acting strange all of a sudden.

We're still staring at one another when the bell over the main door rings, which means a customer has come in. "Listen, I'll reserve the room for next weekend instead. If something comes up, they can always change it," Angie says.

"Sure," Olivia mumbles.

"That makes sense," London agrees.

I just stare at them.

Angie makes the payment for us and then prints out the confirmations. "There you go, all done!" She pats me on the head and leaves the room.

"We'll pay you back in a few days!" I call out.

Back in our booth, Olivia takes out her camera. "Wanna see some pictures?"

I lean forward because of course the answer is yes.

Most of Olivia's pictures are of animals. Usually that's okay with me. But today, I'm obsessed with dogs.

Okay, mostly Candy, because I'm so in love with her already. But also my future dog, the one that will be just mine. I can't wait to see it, hold it in my arms. Snuggle with it. I scroll through the camera. There are a ton of pictures of Candy, looking totally adorable. Most of them are with me. Candy in my arms. Candy sitting on my legs as I spread out in the Pet Room. Candy and me walking side by side in the park.

My grin drops a little bit. "Wow," I whisper. "She's everywhere."

London and Olivia exchange glances. "She is," London says.

"She'll be gone soon," I whisper again.

"Tonight," London agrees quietly. "Uncle Tommy will pick her up after dinner."

Something happens in my stomach. It's like I'm going to throw up or something.

Gross.

The bell above the door rings and we look up. It's Mr. Gordon. "Hey, Dad!" Olivia waves. "What are you doing here?"

He wipes his forehead with a cloth. "Just getting some juice for my men," he replies. "It's hot outside today."

I go back to looking at Olivia's camera. Olivia gets up to talk to her dad, but I hardly notice. When he leaves, she comes back all smiles. She leans over to whisper in London's ear.

That makes me notice. "What are you two talking about?" I ask suspiciously.

"The money for our mom's reservations," Olivia says quickly. But she's looking at her shoes when she says it. Plus, London is biting her lip like she's super nervous about something. I'm almost 100 percent certain Olivia wasn't talking to her dad about spa treatments.

I glare at them. My stomach is churning now. My whole body feels sad and mad and lonely. Just like Candy used to be. Just like a girl whose besties suddenly have secrets she knows nothing about.

Imaan the Lonely. Yup, that's me.

Just like he promised, Uncle Tommy arrives after lunch to take Candy home. And guess what? I absolutely, positively hate that.

"I heard you've been having a good time together," Uncle Tommy says. He's standing in the middle of the Pet Room, watching Candy play with a ball. We'd decided to keep her inside until Mr. Greene could come with his tools to fix the broken wooden piece on the doggy playground.

Candy brings the ball back to me and drops it at my feet. "Good girl," I tell her.

She wags her tail and licks my face. I pick her up for a cuddle.

"Yes, Candy's been so much fun!" London says.

"That's great," he rumbles. "She needed some friends."

I roll my eyes. He never has time for her, so what does he care?

Olivia nudges me when she catches my eye-rolling action. "What's wrong with you?" she whispers.

"Nothing," I say, hiding my face in Candy's fur.

It's weird. I should be happy I'm getting my own dog soon. Instead, I'm as sad and grumpy as Dada Jee without his lemons.

Uncle Tommy clears his throat. "Well, I don't have too much time." He whistles and snaps his fingers at Candy. "We have to go."

I hold Candy tighter. Olivia gives me another nudge, harder this time. "She'll get lonely again," I mumble. It's true. Uncle Tommy has already told us he's too busy for her.

Uncle Tommy sighs loudly. "I have a demanding job," he replies, like that makes it okay.

I'm suddenly angry. "You shouldn't have gotten a dog, then!" I blurt out.

London's eyes bug out. "Imaan!"

I bite my lip. "Sorry," I say, looking down. I don't know what's wrong with me. I shouldn't care this much about Candy. She's just a client. I should focus on the dog that will belong to me soon.

I hope she's small and perfect, just like Candy.

Uncle Tommy shakes his head. "It's okay," he says quietly. "You're right, of course. I work until late at night and on the weekends. And I travel a lot too. It's not fair to a dog."

Candy wiggles out of my grasp and goes over to lick his hand. He pats her head with a little smile. "Look at how happy she is, with kids around her."

"Maybe we can pet sit her again soon?" London offers.

"Yeah, that will be fun!" adds Olivia, clapping her hands. "You can leave her with us every time you have to travel."

I don't say anything. I'm not sure I should talk right now, since I can't trust what comes out of my mouth. Besides, Uncle Tommy looks really sad now too.

"That won't be possible," he says heavily.

"What do you mean?" London demands.

"My company's decided to transfer me to the Las Vegas office," he replies. "Candy's moving."

CHAPTER 17

I miss Candy.

It's Friday evening, and I'm feeling blue. London and Olivia left the day before, soon after Uncle Tommy took Candy and went home. They're not moving to Las Vegas until next month, but it doesn't really matter.

Candy is gone, and I really, really miss her.

"So what do you think?" I ask Dada Jee. We're in the kitchen, making lemonade. It's super easy because I've done this so many times before. Dada Jee cuts the lemons into halves. I squeeze them using our citrus juicer. When an entire jug is full, Dada Jee stirs in water, sugar, and his magical ingredient: a pinch of salt.

Don't ask me why, but salt makes all the difference to a glass of lemonade.

"Well?" I demand. I've just spent the last five minutes explaining the spa getaway to Dada Jee, including how we already reserved everything online and now need to pay Angie back. I know I told my friends that Dada Jee will definitely pay for some of it, but I'm still nervous about asking him. "We're all pitching in, plus London's and Olivia's dads too."

Dada Jee takes a sip of lemonade and nods. "Sure," he says slowly. "I think it's a good idea."

"Yay!" I smile and drink my lemonade. "*Shukriya*, my favorite dada!"

He grunts. "So what kind of dog do you think you'll get?"

My smile fades a little. "I don't know," I say. "Maybe something small, like a terrier."

"Like Candy, eh?" Dada Jee nods, like he knows exactly what I've been thinking.

"Yeah, she was special." I sigh. I wonder what she's doing. Does she have toys in Uncle Tommy's apartment? Is she hiding in her carrier or running around?

Dada Jee goes back to slicing lemons. "Maybe you can get one just like her. Your mama will be happy to have a small, quiet dog in the house."

"Well, I wouldn't say happy, exactly . . ." I begin, a little smile on my lips.

He barks out a laugh. "Yes, I'm not sure what she was thinking, giving in to you like that!"

I pretend to be offended. "What do you mean? I'm responsible, she said so herself!"

He leans over to ruffle my hair. "I'm just joking, Imaan. You've proven to be a very good girl."

I lose my smile immediately. "A good girl with no dad, no pets, and no friends," I whisper.

Okay, I don't really mean that. I'm just being silly. Dada Jee gives me a long look from under his bushy eyebrows. "What's happened to your friends?" he finally asks.

I shrug. "Nothing," I mumble. "Just . . . keeping secrets from me or something."

He opens his mouth to say something, but the doorbell rings. When I see Jake outside, my mouth falls open. "What are you doing here?" I ask, opening the door wider. "Is Pixie all right?"

He grins. "She's great!" He holds out an envelope. "This is for you."

I take the envelope with a frown. "Who's it from? Are you the mail carrier now?"

"Just playing my part," he says mysteriously, then gives me a salute and leaves.

Okay, that was weird. I go back inside to Dada Jee and open the envelope. Inside, there's a thick white paper I recognize from London's special stationery box. The one she only uses for very special occasions.

Your family's presence is requested at the neighborhood park tomorrow at ten o'clock sharp.

I show the paper to Dada Jee and he starts to smile. "Hmmm, maybe those secrets will be revealed tomorrow, eh?"

Maybe.

I toss and turn all night, thinking about the invitation. What could it be? What could be happening tomorrow at the park? Why wouldn't London and Olivia tell me the secret? I'm so curious—and kinda mad—about the whole thing I forget to miss Candy or think about my new dog.

So I guess it worked out. Who needs to be thinking constantly of dogs that belong to other people?

In the morning, I make Mama and Amir dress up after breakfast. "What is this for?" Mama asks, annoyed. "You know I don't have time for nonsense, Imaan."

"I'm sure it's not nonsense, Mama!" I push her toward her bathroom door. "Hurry up, we only have thirty minutes."

I help Amir with his clothes and shoes while Mama showers and changes. Dada Jee is ready when we get downstairs. He's wearing his best trousers and white shirt, with black suspenders over it. "This better be good," he grumbles lightly.

"It will be," I reply. I have no idea what's going on, but I trust London and Olivia. Whatever they've got planned will be good.

"OMG!" I whisper when we reach the park. There's a whole crowd of people gathered in the middle of the open space beyond the swings. Both London's and

Olivia's families are there, plus Mrs. Jarrett and Sir Teddy, Angie, Mr. Bajpai, and Mr. Greene.

My eyes widen when I see Uncle Tommy there too, holding Candy's carrier in his arms. *Why is he here?* I wonder. What is all this?

London waves when she sees us. "Imaan!"

We head to the space in the front. "What's going on?" I ask when we reach her.

She smiles and shakes her head. "You'll see." She turns to Mama. "Mrs. Bashir, stand right here. You four are the guests of honor."

"Cool!" Amir says loudly, making everyone laugh.

I fidget, but we stand like London tells us. Mama, then Amir, then me and Dada Jee. Mama says something to Mrs. Harrison, but I can't hear her. I'm guessing she's asking what's going on. Mrs. Harrison shakes her head.

Wow, everyone's keeping secrets from their besties these days. What's the world coming to?

Just then, Mr. Gordon walks to the front, facing us. As I look at him, I realize he's standing in the place where he and his crew were planting trees earlier. It's near the fence, where Baba and I used to sit.

"Friends, thank you for joining us," Mr. Gordon says. "As you know, I've recently taken on the job of president of the Silverglen beautification committee. We're trying to make this park and the neighborhood pretty and clean for everyone to enjoy."

A few people clap. He nods and goes on. "I was approached by my daughter, Olivia, and her friend London recently. They had an idea for me. They told me a story about a family that's been living here in this neighborhood for years. The Bashir family. There's Imaan, who Olivia and London know very well, but there's also her mother and grandfather, and of course her little brother, Amir. They're all here today. Please give them a round of applause."

Wait, what?

The crowd starts clapping again, and my churning stomach is back. Why is everyone clapping for us? What did we do?

Mama stands ramrod straight, not looking at anyone. I know she's embarrassed and maybe even a little angry. Mrs. Harrison grabs her hand and squeezes.

That's what best friends are for, I guess.

"But there's one person in that family who's not here anymore. It's Imaan's father, Zahid Bashir, who passed away four years ago of cancer. I asked some people in the neighborhood about him, and he seemed to be an amazing person. Helpful, kind, loving. A good neighbor. A good father and husband."

I choke because it's so true. Baba was all those things.

"A good son too," Dada Jee whispers next to me.

I relax a little. I'm not sure why Mr. Gordon is

talking about Baba, but I like it. I wish more people would talk about him. Celebrate him.

Then Mr. Gordon says almost the same thing, and my eyes pop. "The committee has decided to celebrate Mr. Bashir with a permanent symbol." He steps aside, and for the first time, I notice something covered by a tarp right behind him.

He pulls aside the tarp and I gasp. It's a shiny new bench, painted in black, with a plaque on the back. "'In memory of Zahid Bashir,'" he reads.

I feel like my breath is leaving my body like air from a balloon. "That's Baba!" I say faintly.

Mr. Gordon smiles at me. "Yes, Imaan. I believe you used to sit here with your dad when you were a little girl. I hope you'll sit here again whenever you want to feel close to him."

I have a huge lump in my throat, so I can't reply. I just nod.

The people behind me clap and whistle. Dada Jee hugs me. "Seems like your friends had a good secret, eh?" he says in a rough voice.

"Are you crying, Dada Jee?" I ask quietly. "It's okay if you are, you know."

He shakes his head. "I'm not crying." He pulls me toward the bench. "Let's take a look at this thing, eh?"

We stand in front of the bench and just soak it all in. The sparkling new bench. The words on the plaque. The exact space near the fence where I used to sit.

"It's nice," Dada Jee says, clearing his throat.

I don't say anything. I'm not sure I have words right now.

Soon, Dada Jee pats my hand and steps away to talk to Mr. Gordon. I stay where I am, thinking of Baba and how happy he'd be to see the whole neighborhood celebrating him. Shy but happy.

Just like me.

CHAPTER 18

"Sorry we kept it all a secret from you," London says in my ear.

"We wanted to surprise you," Olivia adds in my other ear.

I put an arm around each of them. "I completely understand."

It's true. I was upset to think they were keeping something from me, but it turned out to be the most wonderful secret in the world. Totally worth all the drama.

"Good," London says. "Time to have some fun!"

We're standing in my backyard now. For some reason, the crowd from the park moved to my house after the bench was revealed. I think Mr. Bajpai and Dada Jee were boasting about the doggy playground they built for Candy, and everyone wanted to see it.

I don't mind. These are all my friends, and they celebrated Baba's memory with me today. If they want to hang out in my backyard and drink lemonade, they're welcome to.

All except Uncle Tommy, who's finally let Candy out of her pet carrier. She's sniffing around the platform, like she's searching for something.

"The baby chicks aren't here today," I say. "That's who she's looking for."

"Poor Candy." Olivia giggles.

"Why is your uncle even here?" I demand, looking at London.

She tips her head to the side. "Ask him yourself."

We turn to see Uncle Tommy and Mama walking toward us. I'd noticed them talk to each other before when we first got back from the park. "What's going on?" I ask.

Uncle Tommy clears his throat. "I wanted to thank you girls again for looking after Candy. She seems like a totally different dog now."

"It's the playground," London replies. "It would put anyone in a good mood."

He shakes his head. "It's everything you girls did. You took care of her. Gave her attention and hugs." He's very sad, like he knows he never did those things himself.

Good. I'm glad he's figured it out. Maybe now he'll spend more time with Candy. "Lots of hugs," I repeat.

"Don't forget music and dancing!" Olivia says, giggling.

"Oh yeah, that was fun too!" London agrees. "Candy loves music."

"She loves kids in general," Uncle Tommy says. "I know she's not happy with me. I don't give her the time and attention she deserves. And now with the move to Las Vegas . . ."

I stare at him when he stops talking. Why is he telling us all this?

Mama coughs behind her hand. "Ahem."

"Oh, yeah," Uncle Tommy says. "So I got to talking with your mom here, and we had a great idea."

I stare at Mama, but she just smiles a little. What's with everyone getting ideas recently? I didn't know Mama even knew Uncle Tommy. "What about?" I ask suspiciously.

Mama clears her throat. "We were wondering . . ." She stops and they exchange glances.

"Yes?" I ask impatiently.

". . . if you'd like to adopt Candy."

Wait, what? Did I hear that correctly? Adopt Candy? Have her as my own dog? See her every day, hug her, kiss her, let her sleep on my bed? I don't know what to say because this sounds like a dream. Maybe I'm still asleep. Maybe . . .

London pinches my arm lightly. "Imaan!"

I let out my breath in a deep whoosh. Okay, not a dream. Everyone's staring at me, waiting for an answer. I squeal. "Of course! Of course of course of course!"

Uncle Tommy grins. "Okay, good. I got scared when you didn't say anything."

"I was too shocked!" I gasp. I turn to Mama. "Are you sure?"

Her smile is bigger now. "Yes, I'm sure. Since you're getting a dog, I think it's best to adopt one we already know well."

OMG! Getting permission for a dog was awesome,

but knowing that dog will be Candy is just . . . incredible! I want to hug every single person who's here, but that would be weird, so I just hug London and Olivia.

"I'm so happy for you," London says.

"Me too," says Olivia. "I know this has been your dream for so long."

That reminds me, I never thanked these two for the surprise they planned with Mr. Gordon. I wait until Mama and Uncle Tommy walk away, then say, "Hey, guys, thanks for the bench. It was the best thing you could have given me."

London scoffs. "Don't expect another birthday present until we're in college."

I roll my eyes because I know she's kidding. She's the best gift giver. "Seriously," I say. "I always wanted to have something to celebrate my dad with. Something of his to share with the world. And now I've got it, thanks to you two."

"You're welcome," Olivia says. "My dad was happy to go along with it."

I feel bad about hating them for keeping a secret from me. I chew on my lip, wondering if I should say anything. Then I remember that secrets suck. "It was awful seeing you two sneak away and whisper together. Like you were best friends, and I was . . . not."

They both stare at me, aghast. "Imaan! We would never!" Olivia says loudly.

London gives me another hug. "Sorry bestie, we didn't mean to make you feel bad. We'll be more careful next time we're planning a surprise."

I roll my eyes. "That's okay. I'm over it."

London and Olivia want to go to the bathroom, so I sit by myself at the edge of the doggy playground to watch Candy. It's strange to think she'll be my dog soon. I want to jump up and down in excitement but also keep the news close to my heart for a little longer.

I guess I'm Imaan the Complicated.

Dada Jee sits down next to me, stretching his legs. "Ah! I can't believe this," he says, and for once his tone is not grumpy at all.

I look at him in surprise. "What don't you believe?"

He waves his cane around. "Everything. All these people who came to the park, who clapped at the memory of your father. And they are here right now, smiling, having fun."

"Smiling is pretty easy, Dada Jee," I tease. "You should try it sometime."

He nudges my shoulder with his. "Not my style."

I poke at his mouth with my fingers. "See, you just push your lips up at the corners, maybe even show your teeth a little bit . . ."

He pushes my hand away, but he's smiling. "I know

how to do it, girl. Just . . . never had much reason to."

I sigh and put my head on his shoulder. "Why not? Aren't we reason enough? Me and Amir? Even Mama a little bit?"

He's quiet for a minute, then kisses the top of my head. "You're right. You're reason enough, all of you."

"Perfection," I reply.

"Perfection," he repeats gruffly.

CHAPTER 19

"When are we giving our moms the spa weekend?" Olivia asks.

She and London have joined me at the edge of the playground. London's got a bag of gummy bears, and she passes it around. I take a handful and chew. "No time like the present," I say cheerfully.

We look around. Mama, Mrs. Harrison, and Mrs. Gordon are sitting on the patio, laughing about something. I go upstairs and bring out the printout and gift certificates Angie gave me.

"What's up, girls?" Mrs. Harrison asks. "Having fun?"

"We're just waiting on some baby chicks to arrive," I tell her with a grin. "Then the party will be complete."

"And pizza," London adds. "No party is complete without pizza."

"Oh, good idea." Mama picks up her phone. "Let me order some."

My stomach is rumbling, even with the gummy bears, so I let her order. When she puts her phone down again, I say, "Mama, we have something for all of you."

Mrs. Gordon raises her eyebrows. "For all of us?"

"Yup!" Olivia claps her hands in excitement. "We have a gift for the three of you. Together."

I hand over the printout and gift certificates with a little bow, like we're on a game show or something. "For being awesome, hardworking, busy moms, you three get a free spa weekend in Palm Springs, California!"

"What?" Mrs. Gordon and Mrs. Harrison say together.

Mama takes the papers and starts to read. "This is . . . wow . . . you girls did this?"

"Plus the dads," London says.

"And granddad," Olivia adds.

I lean down to kiss Mama on the cheek. "I know things have been really loud and noisy in our house lately because of Must Love Pets. You're already stressed out because of your job, and the animals and Amir and everything else too. You never just stop working and relax."

"We want all of you to relax, for once," Olivia adds.

"It's a good idea, but we never have time . . ." Mrs. Harrison begins.

"It's for next weekend," London interrupts. "But you can change the reservation if you're not free."

The three women look at one another. "Well," Mama says. "I never have anything planned for weekends."

"Me neither," Mrs. Gordon says, looking a bit sad.

"This is perfect, then!" I tell them. "You ladies go have fun and relax next weekend. Everything will be fine without you. We have our dads, and Dada Jee."

"And us. We help a lot too!" London chimes in.

Mama pats my arm. "I don't doubt that," she says. "You three are so responsible."

The three moms look at one another seriously. Then Mrs. Harrison gives a little squeal, just like a kid. "Ooh! This is gonna be amazing!"

They start talking loudly about what clothes to bring and which restaurants to eat at in Palm Springs.

London, Olivia, and I grin at one another. Giving someone a surprise gift they really need is the best feeling in the world.

Just then, Mr. Bajpai arrives, orange box full of baby chicks in hand. Rahul is with him.

"The chicks didn't turn into superheroes yet, huh, Rahul?" London teases.

He pouts. "It will happen anytime now. That's why I'm not leaving them alone for even a minute."

Amir rushes up and grabs Rahul's arm. "Come on! Let's play!"

We watch the two run off with the orange box. "He isn't sneezing anymore," London remarks.

I freeze because in all my excitement over Candy's adoption, I'd forgotten that my little brother could possibly be allergic to dogs. My heart sinks like a rock. How could we keep Candy in the house, knowing Amir would be miserable?

Mama shakes her head. "I'm not sure what's going on with him. That's the reason I said yes to Candy's adoption. I'm not sure Amir's allergies are related to her."

"They're not!" London says firmly.

We all stare at her. Olivia, me, plus all the moms. "You can't be sure . . ." I begin.

She takes out a paper from her jeans pocket. It's the one she had earlier in the park when Amir and Rahul were on the swings. "I've been taking notes . . ."

Mrs. Harrison chuckles. "Of course you have."

". . . and it seems to me that Amir is actually allergic to dust and mud. He's only sneezed near animals that spend a lot of time walking around covered in dust. From the park or the farmers' market or something like that."

My whole face brightens up. "This is so true!"

"Plus, Candy is a Yorkshire terrier." London says this with hands wide open, like she's saying, *Ta-da!*

"Okay, so?" I wait for her to explain, because obviously this is big news.

"They're a hypoallergenic breed," London continues. "There's low chance of getting allergies because they don't shed fur, compared to big, hairy dogs like Sir Teddy."

"That means we can keep Candy without feeling bad!" I practically shout.

"Exactly," London agrees. "No feeling bad."

Mama is giving me a shocked look, like she had no idea I was feeling bad about adopting Candy. I shrug at her. I guess that's just me. Feeling bad about anything that hurts another person, especially my family.

CHAPTER 20

"Hey, Candy, come back with that ball!"

I yell as I chase my dog—MY DOG, can you believe it?!—across the house. She's fast. She races out of my bedroom and down the stairs, then down the hallway into the Pet Room.

I follow behind, huffing. "That's not fair," I complain. "You've got four legs. I only have two!"

I slide down to the floor and close my eyes. Chasing animals never gets easy.

Candy shoves the ball into her dog bed in the corner of the room, under the window. She loves balls, especially this yellow one I got her as a welcome-to-your-new-home present. Once she's sure the ball is hidden under her toys, she trots back to me quietly.

"Silly girl," I say. She lies down next to me and puts her head on my lap. It's been weeks since I adopted her, and she's been opening up more and more every day. Candy still loves her quiet time, but she's more friendly and active and loving.

She's amazing.

I pet her head. This is the best feeling, right here. I've been waiting for a dog almost my whole life, it seems. Now that I have Candy, my life is perfect.

"Imaan! Help me!" It's Amir, shouting from the kitchen.

I groan. Okay, maybe my life isn't exactly perfect.

I find Amir standing on a stool near the counter with tears in his eyes. "I spilled it!"

There's a plastic jug lying on its side on the counter,

and lemonade dripping all over the floor. I sigh and get a mop. "It's okay, you made a mistake," I say.

Amir's lip trembles. "I wanted to drink some lemonade."

"I'm sure there's more in the fridge," I say. "Dada Jee was going to sell this batch at the farmers' market tomorrow, so he must have made a lot."

"Okay," he says, sniffing. "Will Dada Jee be mad?"

"I'm sure he will," I say cheerfully. Then I see Amir's face. "Just say sorry to him, and he'll forgive you," I add quickly. "Dada Jee is great like that."

I give him a kitchen towel to wipe the counter with, and go back to mopping the floor. In a few minutes, everything looks as good as new. "See?" I smile at Amir.

"Thanks, Imaan," he replies, and hugs my waist.

Aw, I guess being a big sister has its moments.

The back door opens, and London and Olivia walk in. "Finally!" I say, moving away from Amir. "You're late!"

Olivia waves a tub of ice cream at me. "Sorry. It took us a while to decide which one to bring."

"Mint chocolate chip, of course," London adds.

I give Amir a kiss on the top of his head and tell him to be a good boy. He grins wickedly at me, like there's no way that's happening.

London, Olivia, and I head to my room. When we pass the Pet Room, I snap my fingers to call Candy. "Can we stay here for a minute?" Olivia asks.

I raise my eyebrows. "Sure."

We go inside, and for the first time, I notice that Olivia has a tote bag in her hand. "What's going on?" I ask.

"Nothing," she replies. "I just love this room."

I smile. I love this room too. It's full of memories of all the animals we've taken care of this summer. All the fun we've had. Even the difficult parts of Must Love Pets, like when Sir Teddy went missing or the kittens destroyed Mr. Greene's artwork, are planted in my mind forever. "Do you think we'll pet sit again?" I ask quietly.

"Why not?" says London. "We still have three more weeks of vacation left. Maybe that phone in the hallway will ring again soon."

"Maybe." I turn to the door. "Wanna watch a movie in my room?"

Olivia doesn't move. She's holding her tote bag to her chest now, and looking like she's going to be sick. "Er, hold on a minute," she says, her voice low. "I wanted to show you both something."

She puts her hand into the tote bag and takes out a square. London and I come closer. It's a picture of a dog. "That's Candy," I gasp.

"Yes," Olivia replies, smiling. It's a beautiful shot of my dog running at full speed in the backyard, her tongue hanging out.

"This is *your* picture, right?" London asks. "From your camera?"

She means the pictures Olivia takes on her fancy camera. They come out amazing, like the subjects are right in front of you. Olivia's an incredible photographer, but she doesn't like sharing her work.

Maybe something has changed now. "Is this for me?" I ask.

Olivia nods shyly. "You're always after me to take my photography seriously, so I thought I could try making some prints." Then she pauses with a horrified look on her face. "If you don't like it, I can take it back!"

I snatch the print from her hands. "Nope, I'm keeping it."

Olivia sighs in relief. Then she rummages in her tote bag and takes out several more prints the same size as the first one. My mouth falls open. They're of each of our clients, plus some of their animal friends. Sir Teddy with Flash his squirrel friend on his back. Marmalade eating the weeds in our front yard. The three kittens Missy, Bella, and Clyde crawling around their toys. Doc the bunny hopping on his obstacle course. Jake's parakeet Pixie in her cage. There's even a picture of Rahul's three baby chicks pecking the soil in my backyard.

"OMG!" London breathes.

I'd say the same thing, only I can't even breathe right now. The pictures are magnificent. There's no other word for it. "These are . . . these are . . ." I sputter.

Olivia smiles, satisfied with our reaction. "Thanks. I was thinking we could hang these all up here, in the Pet Room. And if we get more clients, we can keep adding to the collection."

I look at the wall in front of me. It's completely bare, and perfect for this photo collection. "Great idea."

Candy looks up at us and barks, like she totally agrees.

I sling my arms around both of my friends. "I think Must Love Pets was the best idea I ever had."

London rolls her eyes. "Sure, like anybody believes it was your idea."

Olivia laughs. "It doesn't matter. We did it all together. Like besties."

I nod. "Perfection."

Read the latest *wish* books!

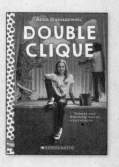

MUST LOVE PETS

GET YOUR PAWS ON ALL THE BOOKS!